D0503864

The
BOOK
of
VIKING
MYTHS

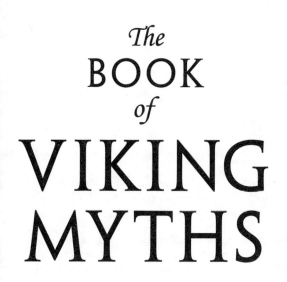

The

BOOK

of

VIKING

MYTHS

From the Voyages of
Leif Erikson to the Deeds of Odin,
the Storied History and
Folklore of the Vikings

PETER ARCHER

Adams Media
New York London Toronto Sydney New Delhi

Adams Media
An Imprint of Simon & Schuster, Inc.
100 Technology Center Drive
Stoughton, MA 02072

For information about special discounts for bulk purchases, please contact Simon & Schuster Special Sales at 1-866-506-1949 or business@simonandschuster.com.

The Simon & Schuster Speakers Bureau can bring authors to your live event. For more information or to book an event contact the Simon & Schuster Speakers Bureau at 1-866-248-3049 or visit our website at www.simonspeakers.com.

Manufactured in the United States of America

9 2023

Library of Congress Cataloging-in-Publication Data has been applied for.

ISBN 978-1-5072-0143-5
ISBN 978-1-5072-0144-3 (ebook)

DEDICATION

For Watson, Vivian, and Frederick. Three Vikings setting out on their voyage of discovery—with a little plundering and pillaging on the side.

ACKNOWLEDGMENTS

Thanks to Karen Cooper, Brendan O'Neill, Rebecca Tarr Thomas, and Katie Corcoran Lytle at Adams Media for their support and assistance with this project. Thanks to Heather Padgen for her superb copyediting. And, as always, thank you to my wife, Linda, for her help and patience.

CONTENTS

Chapter One

WHO WERE THE VIKINGS?

One morning in the year 793, the monks of the monastery of Lindisfarne, off the coast of eastern Britain, looked from their stone huts in puzzlement. A vessel had anchored off the shore, one like none they had seen before. It was long and rode low in the water. Oarsmen maneuvered it into the tiny harbor, while a single square sail hung from the mast in the center of the boat. Its prow rose high above the crew and the monks noticed it was carved into a ferocious dragon's head.

Who were these strange folk? the monks asked one another. And what did they want?

Their questions were soon answered. With cries, the men from the boat leaped ashore, wielding spears and axes. Monks who tried to stop them were hewn down. Others were captured, shackled, and carried off to the ship. Streams of blood ran over the rocks and mingled with the uncaring sea.

The invaders swept through the settlement, seizing precious relics—not for their religious value but for their material worth. When all had been taken or destroyed, the raiders hurled torches into the buildings and returned to their boats. Those monks made captive looked back at the black smoke rising from the holy isle. It was the last they would ever see of it; most of them were carried off to the east where they were sold into slavery.

The raid on Lindisfarne was the first major attack by the people history would come to know as the Vikings. For more than a century, their longboats ranged along the coasts of England, Scotland, and Ireland. They brought such terror with them that for decades priests added to their prayers the words: "From the fury of the Northmen, good Lord, deliver us!" The Lindisfarne raid sent shockwaves throughout Christendom. Alcuin of York, a leading intellectual light of Britain, later a member of the court of Emperor Charlemagne, wrote:

> We and our fathers have now lived in this fair land for nearly three hundred and fifty years, and never before has such an atrocity been seen in Britain as we have now suffered at the hands of a pagan people. Such a voyage was not thought possible. The church of St. Cuthbert is spattered with the blood of the priests of God, stripped of all its furnishings, exposed to the plundering of pagans—a place more sacred than any in Britain.

The first Viking forays were, indeed, almost wholly destructive. What was portable was carried off in the longships. What was not was burned. Monasteries were particularly tempting targets, since they were concentrations of what wealth existed in the early medieval world.

However, gradually, over the next two centuries after the Lindisfarne raid, a change could be discerned. The raiders still came, striking terror into the hearts of Christians. But now they came to stay. Viking settlements spread across northern Britain until by 880 they had captured and controlled more than half the country.

Their territory was called the Danelaw, and their incursions were only halted by the military campaigns of the Wessex ruler, Alfred the Great.

Other Viking bands went even farther afield. Some attacked the coast of France; in 845 a Viking fleet sailed up the Seine River and attacked Paris. Some of the raiders traveled as far east as Baghdad; others launched assaults on the glittering city of Constantinople, the greatest city in Christendom. They penetrated lands to the north and settled there; they were known as Rus, perhaps from the red hair many of them grew. In time, the area would take its name from them and be called Russia.

And, amazingly, they sailed even farther to the west. In 860, Vikings landed on the uninhabited island of Iceland and established a thriving culture there. In the late tenth century Erik the Red, a Viking leader who was, at the time, wanted for murder in Norway and Iceland, planted a settlement in Greenland. Some years later, his son, Leif Erikson, and a small group of companions, sailed still farther west and encountered more land. They called it Vinland; today the site of their first settlement is called L'Anse aux Meadows and lies at the northernmost tip of Newfoundland. It was the first European settlement in North America, coming almost 500 years before the voyages of Columbus.

LEIF THE NEGLECTED

Ironically, Columbus, who came late to the discovery of the New World, is extensively commemorated by city names (e.g., the largest city in Ohio), music ("Hail, Columbia"), and in mnemonic verses ("In fourteen hundred and ninety-two, Columbus sailed the ocean blue"). Leif Erickson, on the other hand, remained largely forgotten until the archaeological discoveries at L'Anse aux Meadows beginning in 1961.

VIKING CULTURE

Although we often associate the Vikings with death and destruction (and they certainly meted out a good bit of both), they also represented a vital and rich civilization. Their art was complex and impressive; they were some of the most skilled seafarers the world has known; and they had a rich and colorful mythology that has left its mark on Western civilization. We call the third day of the week Wednesday after Woden's Day, the fourth day Thursday for Thor's Day, and the fifth day Friday for Frigg's Day. Woden (or Odin, as Scandinavian myth referred to him and as we'll call him in this book), Thor, and Frigg were all important Scandinavian deities. The northerners left us a host of common words: *anger, cog, cozy, flounder, glove* . . . The list goes on and on.

The word "Viking" itself has never been fully explained, but many scholars believe it is derived from the Old Norse word *vik*, which means "to wander." The marauding bands came from Scandinavia, from the kingdoms of Sweden, Denmark, and Norway. Historians argue about what precipitated the migrations, but there is a general consensus that improvements in shipbuilding technology contributed to them. Some also suggest that there were several centuries of global warming that improved chances of children surviving the harsh northern winters. This, in turn, meant more population pressure and more young people available for roaming.

One event may have contributed more than others: in 872 at the sea battle of Hafrsfjord, Harald Fairhair defeated a coalition of Norse noblemen and succeeded in making himself king of Norway. In the aftermath of the battle, many nobles fled overseas to establish their own settlements. This seems to have precipitated many of the raids on France, including an 885 siege of Paris. Other Norwegians sailed to Ireland and effectively took over the country, ruling it until 1014, when they were defeated at the Battle of Clontarf by the great chieftain and Irish hero Brian Boru.

Perhaps the best reason for the Viking explosion was the most straightforward: shipbuilding. In 1903 a Viking ship, known as the Oseberg ship, was discovered at Slagen in Norway. The ship was remarkably well preserved and, together with other discoveries made during the previous half century, gives us a very clear idea of the nature and capabilities of Viking shipbuilding.

The Oseberg Ship

The most remarkable thing about the Oseberg ship is that it exists at all. Most Viking ships (or other early medieval ships) were made of wood and have rotted away, leaving only their impressions in the dirt. But the Oseberg ship was, more or less, intact. Archaeologists treated it with various solutions and allowed it to dry out before moving it to a museum in the center of Oslo, where it remains today.

The ship dates from about 820. Its hull is twenty-two meters long and about five meters across at the midbeam. Viking ships were powered by rowers—probably eight on each side, although the Oseberg ship has spaces for fifteen oarsmen; that was atypical—as well as by sail. The prow rises to a beautifully carven spiral, whose lines move downward to join in the ship's keel.

Viking boats had extremely shallow draughts, something that enabled their sailors to travel easily in rivers as well as the ocean. A mast rose from the middle of the boat, to which was affixed a square sail. The boat was steered by a tiller at the rear.

Archaeologists have speculated that since the sides of the Oseberg ship are low and its keel is thin it might well have been a ceremonial vessel that confined its travels to the fjords. But the striking thing about all Viking ships is how easily maneuverable they were. Still, travel in them cannot have been entirely pleasant, with blowing foam, biting winds, and little or nothing in the way of shelter. The Vikings relied on the stars for navigation.

Like many Viking ships so far discovered, the Oseberg ship was used as a burial vessel. The bodies of two women were contained in it—probably of significant rank, given the size of the ship. Scholars have connected this burial to a Viking cult of fertility that centered on the goddess Freyja, daughter of the god Njord. The Roman historian Tacitus makes reference to a German goddess, Nerthus, who seems to have been the equivalent of Njord, and whose cult was centered on a sacred grove on an island somewhere in the Baltic Sea. The image of the goddess was kept covered in a wooden wagon. Historian Tony Allan writes:

> When the presiding priest sensed that the goddess herself was present, the wagon would be hitched to oxen and led out through the surrounding countryside. Warriors would lay down their weapons as she passed, for she was an Earth Mother, a goddess of peace. Yet she also inspired fear, for when the wagon returned to the sacred grove, the

slaves who ritually cleansed it were drowned as sacrifices to the goddess in the lake where they carried out the task.

The Oseberg ship site included a wagon with a hitch suitable for oxen. So it seems clear that the Germanic fertility cult continued into the Viking age. We know that the Scandinavians practiced human sacrifice until comparatively late. In 921 an Arab traveler, Ibn Fadlān, witnessed the burial of a Viking chieftain. As part of the burial ritual, a slave girl was strangled after being raised three times standing on a wooden frame.

> The first time they raised her she said, "Behold, I see my father and mother." The second time she said, "I see all my dead relatives seated." The third time she said, "I see my master seated in Paradise and Paradise is beautiful and green; with him are men and boy servants. He calls me. Take me to him."

Viking burial rituals, as recounted by the twelfth-century writer Saxo Grammaticus in *Gesta Danorum* (*Deeds of the Danes*), also included the beheading of a cock, but the significance of this is lost to us. One of the unfortunate circumstances from a historian's point of view is that with the coming of Christianity to the Scandinavian country, most remnants of Viking religious practices were wiped out. Today we have only traces of what was at one time a vital and complex religious culture.

VIKINGS AT PEACE

As the Vikings began to settle in areas they conquered, they brought with them a relatively stable society. It was heavily patriarchal and family oriented. Family, as we'll see, plays an important role in Viking myth. Although the Vikings spread through conquest and were preoccupied by raids, there is no indication that in their own lands they were any more warlike than other medieval societies. Wars, when they were fought, were often local affairs to settle disputes over land or possessions. The Northmen fought a series of wars in England to establish the Danelaw until they at last agreed to a truce after suffering defeats at the hands of Alfred the Great. That many of the Viking settlements in Britain were wealthy is indicated by the Cuerdale hoard, a mass of treasure discovered in 1840 in an area of Lancashire called Cuerdale. The horde includes more than 8,600 items, mostly silver, including coins, amulets, chains, and rings. While some of these were undoubtedly the result of plunder, in other cases, jewelry has been found that portrays Viking gods and goddesses. Clearly, this was a people capable of great artistic expression.

Viking society and its structure will be more extensively discussed in Chapter 3.

THE END OF THE VIKING AGE

By the eleventh century, Viking raids had slowed. The Scandinavians had expanded their territories while at the same time becoming more settled and less aggressive. The last great Viking leader was Harald Hardrada (c. 1015–1066), king of Norway. Before becoming king Harald ranged across Europe, traveling to Russia and then in 1034 to Constantinople, where he and his band of followers joined the imperial guard. He raided the Danes for a time before becoming king of Norway in 1046.

The eleventh century saw great changes in Europe, none more so than in Britain. In 1066, the English king Edward the Confessor died, the throne passing to Harold Godwinson. Harald Hardrada saw opportunity here, and invaded England. Although his forces were initially successful in conquering the countryside in the north, Harold Godwinson rushed north with an army and defeated Harald at the Battle of Stamford Bridge. Harald was killed during the battle.

Harold Godwinson's troubles were not over. The following month, an army led by Duke William of Normandy (also called the Bastard) landed on England's south coast. Harold's forces met them at Hastings, and for a time the Anglo-Saxon shield wall held back Norman charges. Then William ordered his archers to loose their arrows high in the air. One struck Harold in the eye. In a panic, the Anglo-Saxons broke ranks, and the Norman knights charged the shield wall and dispersed them. The Norman conquest of England had begun.

From the viewpoint of the Viking age, there is a curious completeness to this. The Normans were, in fact, Viking descendants, whose name derives from "Northmen." So the Norman conquest of England in one sense completed the long process that began in the abbey of Lindisfarne. The Vikings, at last, were triumphant.

Chapter Two

VOYAGES ACROSS THE SEAS

T he power of the Vikings came from their seamanship and, as we discussed in the previous chapter, their shipbuilding abilities. In this chapter we will look briefly at some of the more spectacular voyages they made, ranging over the seas to almost all corners of the earth.

LEIF ERIKSON AND THE VOYAGE TO AMERICA

Among the most incredible of Viking achievements was one that probably meant little to most Scandinavians when it happened: Leif Erikson's voyage to America. This journey, unplanned as far as one can tell, was only verified in the 1960s with the discovery of the remains of Leif's initial settlement.

Sometime in the 980s, an Icelander named Erik the Red killed several men in a dispute about some slaves. Erik had a violent heritage; his father, Thorvald, had come to Iceland, fleeing Norway, where he had killed a neighbor. Icelandic society might have levied one of several penalties against Erik:

- His property could be confiscated, and he could be forced to live apart from society; the term for this is *skógarmathr*, or "man of the forest." Others would be prohibited from helping him leave the country. Should he leave the country, he could be slain without penalty against whoever did the killing.
- He might be exiled (*herathsseket*) from his district for a given length of time.

Erik's crime was considered serious enough (although not of the most serious type) that he was sentenced to exile for three summers, in addition to a fine. Erik settled on an island off the coast where he again became involved in a quarrel with neighbors and killed several of them. This time the court decided that Erik should be subject to *skógarmathr*, the most severe criminal penalty it could impose.

Never one to bow to authority, Erik and his men at once began planning to leave the country.

Some time prior to these events, a Viking sailor, blown off course, had sighted land to the west and north of Iceland, although he had not landed there. Now Erik was determined to follow up on this sighting and to found his own colony. His adventures are described in *Erik's Saga*.

THE VINLAND SAGAS

Erik's Saga and the *Grœlendinga Saga* are collectively known as the Vinland Sagas. They were composed separately sometime in the thirteenth century, although scholars believe they are based on an earlier oral tradition, since they are less consciously literary than other sagas of the Scandinavians. They tell the story of Erik the Red's journey to Greenland from Iceland and of Leif Erikson's voyage to North America, which he called Vinland.

Erik and his followers set sail and after a voyage lasting some months landed on the coast of a large body of land that stretched to the north and west. Rather than remain in the place of their first landing, the Icelanders sailed along the coast, rounding the southern end of the land and going some distance north along its west coast. Eventually, they founded two settlements: Brattahlid at the southern end of what they were now calling Greenland, and Lysefjord, farther north.

LEIF ERIKSON

Erik's son Leif was born in Iceland sometime during the 970s and grew up accustomed to travel in the ships of his father. Erik himself seems to have been too busy to pay much attention to his son, and Leif was largely raised by one of Erik's followers, a man named Tyrker.

In 999, Leif and a band of men set out for Norway. They were blown off course and ended up wintering in the Hebrides, islands off the coast of Scotland. Eventually, they reached Norway where they became part of the retinue of the great Norse king Olav Tryggvason. Olav succeeded in converting Leif to Christianity, though Leif, according to *Erik's Saga*, was reluctant to abandon the gods of his fathers. The king, perceiving Leif's strength of character, gave him the mission of returning to Greenland to convert its inhabitants to the new faith.

> The king said he saw no man more suitable for the job than Leif—
> "and you'll have the good fortune that's needed."

Leif and his followers set sail for their home. Again, the weather for the crossing was unfavorable, and they were "tossed about at sea for a long time."

> He chanced upon land where he had not expected any to be found.
> Fields of self-sown wheat and vines were growing there; also there
> were trees known as maple, and they took specimens of all of them.
>   Leif also chanced upon men clinging to a ship's wreck, whom he
> brought home and found shelter for over the winter. In so doing he
> showed his strong character and kindness.

Vinland

The land that Erik had found he called Vinland, from the number of vines he found growing. There is some dispute about where exactly it was. One group of archaeologists has argued for L'Anse aux Meadows on the northern tip of Newfoundland. It is clear from ruins discovered there in the 1960s that the area was settled by Norsemen, and it has generally been identified with a settlement by Leif, which was later called Leifsbudir (Leif's Booths). However, one thing that militates against this being the place described in *Erik's Saga* is the fact that the area around L'Anse aux Meadows is completely bare of vines and the other vegetation. A more likely candidate is the area around the entrance to the St. Lawrence Seaway, where there is also evidence of a Viking settlement.

Whatever the case, it is interesting that the Vikings showed no interest in colonizing the new land as they had done with Iceland. In truth, Leif's discovery came as the Viking age was drawing to an end. North America would remain free from further European incursion for another 500 years.

THE DANELAW

Beginning in the eleventh century, the northern and eastern sections of England were formally known as the Danelaw. Although the term signaled the recognition by the Anglo-Saxons that a permanent Scandinavian presence had been established in Britain, it was in fact the result of a defeat for the Vikings.

The Battle of Edington

Since the first raid on Lindisfarne in 789, Viking activity along the shores of Britain had been steadily increasing. In 865, the *Anglo-Saxon Chronicle*, our primary source for this period, records the coming of a "great heathen army" led by Ivar the Boneless and his brothers Ubba and Halfdan. This army succeeded in conquering a large area as one by one the various Anglo-Saxon kingdoms collapsed. In 870, the Vikings fought the men of Wessex in the Battle of Merton, during which the West Saxon king Æthelred was killed. He was succeeded by his brother Alfred.

Of all the Anglo-Saxon rulers who preceded the Norman conquest of 1066, Alfred is unquestionably the best known—primarily for his activity in opposing the Viking forces threatening Wessex. Yet he lost the first few battles he fought against them, and by the winter of 877–78 he had been driven into a marshy area in present-day Somerset. There he plotted his strategy to halt the invaders. In the spring of 878 he gathered his followers and met the Vikings at Edington.

Guthrum, leader of the Viking horde, occupied the town and waited, as usual, for a large ransom payment to be made before moving on. In May, he met Alfred's forces. According to Asser's *Life of Alfred*:

> Fighting ferociously, forming a dense shield-wall against the whole army of the Pagans, and striving long and bravely, through God's will, at last [Alfred] gained the victory.

The resulting peace treaty accomplished two important things. First Guthrum agreed to convert to Christianity. Second, he agreed that a boundary should be established between the lands controlled by the Danes and those ruled by Alfred.

Cnut the Great

The most important ruler of the Danelaw was Cnut the Great (c. 995–1035). In a military campaign that climaxed in 1016 he succeeded in doing what other Danish rulers had not and captured London. He and the English king Edmund negotiated a treaty that granted Cnut rule over all the land north of the Thames River. When Edmund died that winter, by the terms of the treaty Cnut became king of all England. Among his first acts was to levy an enormous tax (the Danegeld), which he used to pay off his army.

KIEV AND THE RUS

According to the *Annals of St-Bertin*, in 839 a delegation from the Byzantine emperor Theophilus at Constantinople (modern-day Istanbul) arrived at the court of King Louis the Pious, king of Aquitaine, to negotiate a treaty of peace between the two monarchs. Attached to the delegation were a group of men who called themselves Rus. They asked Louis for safe conduct through his territory, as they were returning to their own homes.

Louis distrusted them, particularly when he discovered that the homes to which they were returning were in Sweden; people living in Aquitaine had learned over the past half century to be wary of people from Scandinavia. Accordingly, the king indicated that he would detain them for a time and if he found nothing against them, he would give them the safe conduct they were requesting. The story ends there, and we don't know if the Rus were sent on their way or spent the rest of their lives languishing in prison in Aquitaine. But it is significant as being the earliest mention of the Rus.

WHY "RUS"?

Scholars have suggested several reasons for the name Rus. One suggestion is that the Swedes came from Roslagen, an area north of Stockholm. Another is that it is related to the Finnish word *ruotsi*, which means "men who row." It is also possible that it relates to their red hair.

Attacks Across the Baltic

There was a long tradition of Scandinavian piracy and attacks across the Baltic Sea. Snorri Sturluson, in the *Ynglingasaga*, mentions a Swedish king named Sveigdir who traveled across the sea in search of Godheim (God Home) and Odin the Old. He searched for five years, during which he traveled as far as Turkey "and found there many kinsmen." Accepting Snorri's account as at least possibly accurate, there appears to have been a Scandinavian migration east as well as west.

The Danish historian Saxo Grammaticus in *Gesta Danorum* describes Viking raids being carried out in Baltic countries in the 840s and 850s by Ragnar Lodbrok and Hasting. However, such raids had one significant obstacle: There were no rich monasteries to plunder.

SAXO GRAMMATICUS

The writer known as Saxo Grammaticus (c. 1150–c. 1220) was possibly a secretary to a prominent Danish archbishop. In this position, he would have been well placed to observe goings on at the Danish royal court. His *Gesta Danorum*, besides being a valuable written source for the events of the Viking age, is also notable as offering an early version of the story of Hamlet, prince of Denmark.

Instead, the Viking goal seems to have been to find passage to Constantinople and the rich trading possibilities it offered. They were aided by three large rivers: the Western Dvina, the Dnieper, and the Volga. Viking ships were admirably suited for river travel, being of shallow draft and easily steerable. By the 830s, there was a Viking settlement on Lake Ladoga east of the Gulf of Finland. From there it was possible to travel by river (albeit on smaller boats than those they had used to cross the Baltic) south to the Black Sea.

Such river routes were still insecure in the first part of the ninth century; hence the fact that the Rus at the Aquitanian court had traveled north with a group of other people. However, the Rus found an important instrument in securing them: the Kievan, or Old Russian, state.

Kiev

According to the *Russian Primary Chronicle*, a compilation made in the twelfth century, the people living along the Dnieper River resisted an attempt by a tribe called the Varangians, whom scholars generally identify with the Rus, to impose a tribute on them. Although the local tribes resisted and drove the Varangians back, they proved incapable of governing themselves. A period of conflict ensued, and in the end representatives of the various tribes traveled to Sweden and asked the Rus, or Varangians, ("just as some of them are called Swedes, and others Normans, Angles, and Goths," says the *Chronicle*) for leaders who would unite them and protect them. The Rus provided three leaders: Rurik, Sineus, and Truvor. Sineus and Truvor were soon dead, leaving Rurik as the sole leader. Rurik established his capital at Novgorod, which became known as the Kingdom of the Rus.

The Rus now controlled the trade route along the Volga. They expanded south, capturing the city of Kiev and founding the medieval Kievan state. From here they fought various wars with the Byzantine Empire as well as engaging in trade with it. Although their culture did not last, their name did, and eventually the expanding polity was given the name Russia.

NORTHMEN AND NORMANDY

In the 850s when the Vikings sailed up the Seine and besieged Paris, they had been attacking the Frankish coastline for more than three decades. The first attacks came in 820 around the mouth of the Seine and continued, involving increasing numbers of the Northmen.

In 857 two Viking warrior captains, Sigtrygg and Bjorn, joined forces. Having previously fought their way up the Seine as far as Chartres, this time they captured and sacked the town and its great cathedral and then attacked Paris. The two armies continued to raid the area, culminating in 876 when a fleet of 100 ships sailed up the Seine. This time, though, there was no attack; the Vikings were bought off by a bribe from King Charles the Bald of 5,000 livres. This did not, however, stop the Vikings from attacking the church at Bayeux and killing the bishop.

It was evident to the Frankish monarchy that these raids would continue indefinitely. The 5,000 livres represented nothing more than a temporary halt. Next time, the attacks would be more severe and the amount required to stop them would be greater. Clearly a different sort of approach was required. To that end, they decided to offer not money but land.

Rollo of Normandy

The ancestry of the Viking chieftain who was to found the colony of Normandy is uncertain. There is evidence that he took part in the attack on Paris in 876. At some time subsequent to this, he captured the city of Rouen, defeating the Franks by pretending to order his men to flee to their boats; when the Franks pursued them, the city's defenders fell into concealed pits dug by Rollo's men. The Vikings thereupon turned back upon those remaining and slaughtered them so effectively that they were able to enter the city unopposed.

It was the completeness of this victory, evidently, that motivated King Charles the Simple to invite Rollo to negotiate a grant of land from the Frankish king. The actual treaty was signed in 912 and gave the Viking chief a large tract of land in northwestern France. In return for this, Rollo agreed to convert to Christianity and to join the king in defending the Kingdom of the Franks from other aggressors.

It was an ingenious solution that belies Charles's name. By giving motivation for the Vikings to settle down and stop raiding, Charles also enlisted a powerful fighting force in his service, one that could range far afield if need be. A second grant of land in central Normandy was given to Rollo in 924. He died somewhere around 933, and afterward a third grant of land was given to his son, William Longsword.

The Vikings had now succeeded in forcing three negotiated truces with European kingdoms: the treaty of 878 between Alfred the Great of Wessex and Guthrum that created the Danelaw; agreements negotiated in the early tenth century between the Byzantine emperor and the Kievan Rus; and King Charles's grant of Normandy to Rollo. Although none of the Viking states would survive, their cultural influence was immense.

The Importance of the Normans

Although Normandy is probably associated in most minds today with World War II and the events of June 6, 1944, it played an important role in history long before that. It was, of course, the jumping-off point for William the Conqueror's 1066 expedition to seize the English throne. By that time, only a bit more than a century since the establishment of the Norman duchy, the Viking founders had changed their religion, their warlike habits, and their language. They now were Christian and spoke an early form of French.

ENGLISH AS A HODGEPODGE

The English language is peculiar from a linguistic standpoint in that it is an amalgam of two distinct branches of the Indo-European family of languages: Germanic and Latinate. Before 1066, Old English was closely related to Old Norse, a Germanic language; the resemblance was even greater in the north, where there was a preponderance of Scandinavian words as a result of the Danelaw.

After 1066, Old French, a Latinate language (that is, derived from Latin) became the dominate language. The two languages, Old French and Old English, gradually merged, but even today a majority of the words in English have Latin roots rather than Germanic ones.

Although they no longer raided and plundered, the Normans still retained expansionist tendencies. The invasion of England is one example. Somewhat earlier, in the 1050s, a swashbuckling Norman noble named Roger and his brothers led an expedition to Sicily. There they began a campaign of conquest. By 1091, they held the entire island, which became the Kingdom of Sicily, which would last until 1816. The Normans, like their Viking forebears, ranged widely throughout Europe, often serving as mercenaries to various monarchs.

Chapter Three

LIFE AMONG THE VIKINGS

Although our image of the Vikings is as seagoing folk, always sailing toward their next raid, as previous chapters have made clear, beginning in the ninth century they began to form permanent settlements in many of the lands they had raided. This was where they set out from on new voyages of discovery and conquest; this was where, gathered around the fire, they told stories of the gods and their deeds. But what did these settlements look like?

HUNTING AND FARMING

The first requirement of any permanent settlement was, of course, a reliable source of food. The Vikings were accomplished hunters and fishermen, but they also brought with them knowledge of farming. Where soil was good and the climate was favorable, they planted crops and raised domesticated animals. Horses were of particular importance, both as a means of transportation and of cultivating the land. This goes a long way toward explaining the prominence of horses in Viking mythology, beginning with Odin's eight-legged steed Sleipnir.

Archaeological investigation of Viking sites during the past century shows they supplemented their food with honey, eggs, and various wild plants. A surviving poem, the *Rígsthula*, describes a farmer as having tamed oxen, constructed ploughshares, built houses and barns in which to store hay, and created carts for hauling his crops.

THE *RÍGSTHULA*

This poem survives in a single version as part of the fourteenth-century Codex Wormianus, which also contains a version of the *Prose Edda*. For its account of the doings of the god Ríg, see Chapter 9.

Horses or oxen could be used to drag the plough, a simple arrangement with an iron blade to turn over the soil. On smaller plots, a man might have to push or pull the plough himself until he could save enough money to purchase an animal. Wheat was cut with a sickle mounted on a pole, as it was in the rest of Europe. When it was ready, it was ground, usually by hand, into flour and then baked into bread.

Animals were hunted or sometimes slaughtered, particularly those not expected to survive the harsh northern winter. The meat could then be cut into long strips, salted, and dried in the sun or over the fire. Cows were often turned out to pasture in wheat fields where the wheat had been cut down. In some areas such as Norway, the practice developed of driving herds of sheep and cows into the uplands during the summer and into the lowlands during the winter.

Larger farms were worked by a combination of slaves—who might be men who had incurred some debt they were unable to pay off or prisoners captured in a raid—and free laborers. Women and children were employed in cloth weaving and other domestic pursuits, although in times of harvest they, too, would labor in the fields to get the crops in.

TRAVEL AND TRADE

The Vikings were, as we've seen, superb sailors. But what about during winter, when the fjords in Scandinavia or the waterways of Britain and Ireland froze? Farming communities could become completely isolated from the rest of the world, and their inhabitants had to hope that they had managed to put aside enough food and fuel for the winter. Unquestionably each winter some of these communities found they had miscalculated and did not survive.

However, some limited travel was possible during the winter. Archaeologists have found iron spikes that could be mounted on horses' hooves to give them purchase on ice. Skates made from bone could be used to traverse frozen lakes, rivers, or inlets.

Barter was absolutely necessary to Scandinavian farming life. Although a farm might be able to grow enough food to feed its inhabitants, such things as tools, cloth, or jewelry might very well be obtained through barter. And, of course, such things could also be brought back after raids on non-Viking communities.

As the Vikings expanded to the east, especially after the founding of the Kievan state, they increased trade contacts as far afield as

Constantinople. Although they retained much of their warlike character, the Vikings in this part of the world became increasingly involved in commercial activities. Over time, goods from the east made their way steadily west, traveling as far as Iceland.

VIKINGS AT HOME

Some of the best evidence we have for what Viking society looked like comes from the southern Danish village of Hedeby. One reason for this is that rising sea levels covered much of the town, and water is a great preserver of wood. Since the houses in the town were made of wood, remnants of them have survived in greater numbers than elsewhere.

Houses were built from what is called stave construction. Wooden slats were driven into the ground to form a continuous wall, and buttresses were placed on the outside to prop it up and keep it from collapsing outward under the weight of the roof. The roof itself was thatched with straw, with a hole left for smoke from the fire to escape.

The inside of the house was simplicity itself. An earthen bench was built up, held in place by wooden boards. Here the family could sit or sleep. In some cases, actual benches were constructed. One was found on the Oseberg ship.

In places such as Ireland or Iceland or the outer islands of Scotland where there were few or no trees, houses were constructed of stones, dry-laid on one another. Turf walls might also be laid on a stone foundation, and the roofs were of turf.

Such homes were necessarily small and cramped, with little space for each inhabitant. Family life was a distinctly intimate affair, with parents, children, and grandparents almost piled on top of one another. In summer, the family would be out and about, tending to crops and animals, but in winter they spent many weeks indoors by the fire. To pass the time, they told stories.

FURNISHINGS

Furnishings for Viking houses were naturally simple; there wasn't a great deal of room for externals. The focus of the family was the hearth, on which they burned wood or peat.

WHAT IS PEAT?

Peat is dug from bogs or marshy, damp areas. It is decayed vegetation that has compacted into a solid mass. When it is dried out, it can be used as a fuel, which smolders rather than burning. The result is that a peat fire, while not producing much in the way of flame, can be a long-term source of heat while consuming fuel much more slowly than a wood fire.

The single most important cooking utensil in the house was the cauldron, which was suspended over the fire from a spit. In the cauldron, the inhabitants could cook stews or soups. As we will see, Viking mythology makes prominent use of cauldrons, particularly a magical cauldron that is an endless source of food. Generally cauldrons were made from iron, but some have been found that were carved from soapstone with iron handles.

The spit could also be used to roast meat, which was cut with iron knives and eaten with the fingers. Spoons for stirring the pot could be carved from wood. Food was stored in clay pots. Fish and meat could also be cooked by putting them in a hole in the ground and surrounding them with hot stones.

Generally, the Vikings grew barley and rye, which they made into bread. They also brewed strong beer from these grains and fermented honey to create mead. Mead was a common drink and appears often in Viking myths, most notably in the Mead of Poetry, stolen by Odin for the gods. Milk was obtained from goats or cows. Wine was acquired through trade or raiding (many monasteries in Britain had vineyards). As a precious commodity its consumption was confined to the upper classes.

Weaving

In addition to their other responsibilities, Scandinavian women were responsible for weaving wool into cloth. Drop spindles were used more than spinning wheels because of their compactness and the ease of making them. The looms were upright, and a skilled weaver could weave enough cloth during a long winter to cloth her entire family. Large numbers of artifacts have been found at Viking sites that show how elaborate was the process of weaving, dying, and caring for clothing. In addition, cloth had to be woven for the sails so essential to Viking longboats.

Games

In addition to telling stories, drinking, and probably fighting with one another, Vikings had other ways of passing the time. Archaeologists have found wooden or stone game boards with game pieces something like marbles. Chess had spread to the outer islands of Scotland by the twelfth century and was probably there earlier, so it is possible that at least some of the Vikings were familiar with it.

THE LEWIS CHESSMEN

In 1831, a group of chess pieces were discovered on the Island of Lewis in the Outer Hebrides off the coast of Scotland. Current feeling among scholars is that at least some of them were made in Trondheim, Norway.

THE DEVELOPMENT OF TOWNS AND TRADE

Early in the Viking age, small settlements were the norm. But as the Vikings spread farther and farther afield and began to expand their trading with other civilizations, there was a growth of urban areas. This may seem incongruous—who thinks of "Vikings" and "city dwellers" together?—but the fact is that expanded commerce demanded the formation of towns and cities. For example, in 873 by arrangement with the king of the Franks, Vikings settled for a time on an island in the Loire River and traded with neighboring communities.

One of the contributing factors to this was the establishment of formal tributes to the Vikings from places they had raided. We would think of this as protection money, a guarantee that the towns or settlements would be free from Viking incursion, provided the tribute was paid promptly. This meant that large amounts of money were injected into the Viking economy on a regular basis. Between 991 and 1014, the Vikings received more than 150,000 pounds of silver as part of the arrangement in England establishing the Danelaw (see Chapter 2). Scandinavian countries struck their own coins, which were mingled in Viking hoards with those of many other nations.

Trade Goods

Coinage helped the Vikings obtain many things they were unable to make for themselves: good, strong weapons such as swords made from some other metal than iron, which tended to be brittle; pots, pans, and other luxury cooking utensils; well-woven cloth from the east. All of these goods circulated through those areas inhabited by the Vikings, passing west as far as Iceland.

In exchange, the Vikings were able to inject into the economic bloodstream of medieval Europe many goods that were previously scarce, including slaves, furs, and walrus tusks. The Vikings' steady raiding in Britain, Ireland, and elsewhere ensured them a copious supply of captives who could be sold off as slaves in Kiev, the Byzantine Empire, and elsewhere.

Archaeological excavations in Sweden, Norway, and Denmark show that the presence of traders worked both ways. Not only did the Vikings travel east with boatloads of goods and silver coins, but merchants from the east began to travel west in increasing numbers. All of this meant the spread of not just goods but culture. Images of Thor and Odin spread across Europe, accompanied by Viking tales of these and other gods and heroes.

Towns

Towns are focal points for trade in any society. They concentrate the population and make it possible for economic structures to grow and expand. There was a proliferation of towns during the Viking age.

Scholars study Hedeby, mentioned previously, as a typical town during the height of the Viking period. It was penetrated by a stream, which ran through its middle and served as both a source of drinking water and as something that could carry away waste products. The stream emptied into the ocean, and in the harbor the people of Hedeby built a number of piers to accommodate numerous ships that docked there.

Running from the sea and back again in a semicircle around the town was an earthen wall that originally was between twenty and thirty feet fall. This, in turn, was surrounded by another, outer, wall. Thus the town was protected on three sides by the wall and on one by water. Nonetheless, despite this impressive defensive system, the town was destroyed several times in the eleventh century. After the last time, the inhabitants decided not to rebuild it, and the town sank into ruin. The sea rose, covering much of the town's buildings, preserving them for posterity.

VIKING WEAPONS

Because so much of Viking life was wrapped up with battles, raids, and warfare, it is important to understand as much as we can about how they fought and what they fought with. Fortunately, quite a lot of information is available concerning this. In particular, the custom of burying warriors with their weapons makes it possible to understand how the Viking fighting habits and equipment evolved over the centuries.

Although the popular image is of Vikings wielding axes, the Norse warrior was more inclined to use swords and spears. Swords, usually made of iron, were at first single edged but then changed to double-edged weapons with a low ridge running down the middle of the blade for balance. They were carried in scabbards, and the hilts of the swords as well as the scabbards often contained complex and beautiful decorations. Special swords, or, in myth, magical swords, were given their own names. Given that swords were expensive and that the best swords were generally obtained in trade, it was not unusual for an especially prized weapon to be passed down from father to son over several generations.

Spears might be for hurling, in which case they were javelins and were relatively light. These were helpful in battles at sea with other long-boats, since they could be thrown at the opposing crew and warriors to disable them. Spears that were intended for fighting at close quarters were heavier both in the head and the staff.

Axes were used in battle and are not that much different from the domestic tool. They had broad blades and were superbly balanced. The disadvantage of an axe as opposed to a sword was that the latter could be used for both thrust and parry.

Warriors carried large wooden shields, brightly decorated, that might stop arrows or all but an especially vigorous blow from an axe or a sword. Apart from that, armor was limited. Warriors wore conical helmets, often with pieces hanging down to protect the nose and ears (see Chapter 13 on the hoard at Sutton Hoo).

Battles

Before a battle (as opposed to a raid such as the one that destroyed Lindisfarne in 793), the leader of the Viking army would give a speech to his followers to raise their adrenaline and prepare them for the battle ahead. Given the size of some Viking armies—1,000 to 1,500 men in some cases, standing on a windy plain—it seems likely that only the front ranks could hear the words spoken and repeated them to warriors standing behind them. Warriors also hurled insults at one another; the rich tradition of Viking insults is reflected in many of the stories in the Eddas in which gods and men hurl epithets and charges of cowardice at one another.

Siege machines were not unknown, although the Vikings rarely laid siege to towns. The siege of Paris in the ninth century was an exception, probably prompted by anticipating of the riches for the taking that lay within the city.

All in all, the Vikings were formidable warriors, but during the Viking age they also evolved a steady and productive life as farmers, traders, and townspeople.

Chapter Four

THE SOURCES OF VIKING MYTHOLOGY

We are fortunate in having a large amount of source material from which to study Viking mythology, but one source stands out. In the thirteenth century, a native of Iceland, Snorri Sturluson, composed the work that has come down to us as the *Prose Edda*. This book gives us the most complete account of the Viking gods and goddesses and some of the chief stories associated with them.

SNORRI STURLUSON

Snorri Sturluson (1179–1241) was an important figure in Iceland. The nation had no king but instead was governed by an assembly of its prominent figures, the Althing. Snorri was twice chosen lawspeaker of the assembly. Snorri was born into a high-ranking family but was raised by Jón Loftsson, called by some historians the "uncrowned king of Iceland." It seems that Snorri's father, Sturla, was in dispute with another nobleman when that nobleman's wife lunged at him with knife. Although Sturla merely suffered a cut on the cheek, he demanded excessive compensation. Loftsson settled the dispute by agreeing to bring up Snorri as his son, thus elevating him still further in Icelandic society.

Snorri evinced interest early on in Scandinavian myths. After his first election as lawspeaker in 1215, he traveled to Norway where he was a guest of King Hákon Hákonarson, who hoped to extend his rule to include Iceland. Snorri also, through other connections, became acquainted with the history of Sweden. Thus when he returned to Iceland, he had an unusually broad knowledge of Scandinavian history and culture. He was also what we would call today an agent of influence on behalf of the Norwegian king. Snorri was elected again to the position of lawspeaker in 1222. He came into increasing conflict with other Icelandic chiefs over the issue of his allegiance to Norway, and by 1238 Hákon Hákonarson no longer regarded him as reliable. Snorri visited Norway again, and this time the king attempted to detain him there. Snorri made his way back to Iceland in 1239, but now he was alienated from most of the other chiefs. In 1241, a plot was concocted to assassinate him, and in autumn of that year it was carried out. Snorri was cornered in the basement of his house and struck down as he begged the assassins not to strike.

THE *PROSE EDDA*

Snorri's most important work, the *Prose Edda*, is remarkable on several counts. First, it contains a relatively systematic explanation of Scandinavian myth. Second, Snorri suggests that the gods of Viking mythology began as real human beings whose deeds were remembered and around whom cults formed until they were gradually transformed into gods. Thus he recounts that Odin and Thor were both originally of Trojan stock and that Odin traveled to Scandinavia where his offspring became rulers and fathers of the various peoples of the region.

EDDA

The meaning of the word *edda* is obscure. The *Prose Edda* was written in Old Icelandic (a branch of Old Norse), and in that language the word means "great-grandmother." Since the original of Snorri's manuscript has been lost, it's not even clear that he himself used that word in the title of the work.

The Structure of the Edda

The *Edda* contains four parts:

1. The Prologue
2. *Gylfaginning* (The Fooling of Gylfi)
3. *Skáldskaparmál* (Poetic Diction)
4. *Háttatal* (List of Meters)

THE *SKÁLDSKAPARMÁL* AND *HÁTTATAL*

These parts of the *Edda* are concerned with the technical forms of Norse poetry. Ostensibly a dialogue between two gods, Bragi and Ægir, about poetic forms, the *Skáldskaparmál* is in fact a long list of kennings—that is, poetic forms in which two words are substituted for a third word to form a metaphor. For example, rather than say "ship," a poet might say, "wave horse," which is more colorful.

In *Háttatal*, Snorri describes various forms of poetic meter, using as examples, his own verses. This section is often omitted from modern versions of the *Prose Edda*.

Of these four parts, *Gylfaginning* and *Háttatal* are the most lengthy.

Gylfaginning presents its information within a framing device—a journey by King Gylfi to Asgard. Gylfi was, Snorri says, "a wise man skilled in magic." He knew of the existence of the race of folk called the Æsir, who were wise in everything. Gylfi determined to find out if this was because of the gods they worshipped, so he disguised himself as an old man and traveled to Asgard, seat of the Æsir.

However, the Æsir, who had the gift of sight, knew that he was coming. They decided to cloak his journey in illusions.

When Gylfi came to Asgard, he saw a great hall, its roof shingled with golden shields. It was so high he had difficulty seeing over it. This hall, he knew, was Valhalla. A man guarded the gate, juggling seven swords. Gylfi, pretending to be a traveler named Gangleri, asked what the hall was.

"It is the dwelling place of our king," replied the man.

"Who might he be?" asked Gylfi.

"Come along," said the man. "I will take you to him, and you can ask him yourself."

They entered the hall, and Gylfi saw three thrones, each higher than the next. A man was sitting in each. The man in the lowest seat, they told him, was called High, while the next highest man was Just-as-High. The third man was called Third.

Gylfi began to question them about the gods, and their answers compose the remainder of the *Gylfaginning*.

THE GOLDEN HALL

Valhalla's golden roof is mentioned in a number of stories. Readers of J.R.R. Tolkien's *The Lord of the Rings*, a book profoundly influenced by northern legends, may recall Meduseld, the home of Théoden of Rohan, which is referred to as the Golden Hall, perhaps a reference to Valhalla.

Gylfi's questioning of the mysterious three Æsir is fairly methodical. He first inquires about the origins of the world, then about the various gods, including Odin the Allfather, Thor, and Loki (who is not a god but spends a great deal of his time annoying the gods). As well, he asks about the lesser gods and goddesses. From there he proceeds to ask about stories concerning the gods.

The three are obliging in their answers, giving long explanations and tales. At last they come to Ragnarök, the end of the world, which they explain to Gylfi in full. When Gylfi asks if Ragnarök will mean the true end of the world or if there is something more, the High tells him briefly of the rise of a new world upon the ashes of the old. "If you know how to ask questions reaching still further into the future," the High tells him, "then I do not know the source of your questions because I have never heard of anyone who could tell events of the world further into the future. And may you find use in what you have learned."

At this point, Gylfi/Gangleri hears noises all around him and realizes he is standing in the midst of a great open plain. There is no sign of the fortress or the hall in which the three Æsir had been sitting. Gangleri returned to his people "where he told of the events that he had seen and what he had heard. And after him, people passed these stories down from one to the other."

The most interesting element in the story, though, is contained in the epilogue in which the Æsir discuss among themselves what occurred. They recollect all the stories they told (and it's implied that they made them up more or less on the spot) to Gangleri.

> Then they gave the same names, mentioned above, to people and places there, so that, after much time had passed, people would not doubt that all were one and the same, that is, those Æsir who have been spoken about and the ones who now were assigned the very same names. Someone there was then called by the name Thor, and he was taken to be the old Thor of the Æsir and Thor the Charioteer. To him they attributed the great deeds that Thor or Hector accomplished in Troy.

Snorri thus further ties the stories of Scandinavian myth to ancient classical myths of Troy. (He also, in a subsequent passage, identifies the crafty Ulysses or Ulixes—Odysseus to the Greeks—with Loki, the trickster god.)

THE *ELDER EDDA*

In the *Prose Edda* Snorri injects numerous quotations from poetic material, much of which is unknown from any other source. Snorri's quotations include:

- *Sayings of the High One*
- *The Sibyl's Prophecy*

- *The Lay of Hyndla*
- *The Lay of Vafthrúdnir*
- *The Lay of Grímnir*
- *The Lay of Fafnir*
- *Loki's Flyting*

Some of this material comes from the *Poetic Edda* (about which more following), but scholars speculate that other elements must come from a source accessible to Snorri that has now been lost; that source has been designated the *Elder Edda*.

THE *POETIC EDDA*

Snorri is by no means our only source for Viking mythology. Equally important is the *Poetic Edda* (so called to distinguish it from Snorri's book).

Although the *Poetic Edda* was written in the thirteenth century, the materials it assembles and draws on are much older, many probably predating the rise of the Vikings. It is not known who assembled the *Poetic Edda*, though several candidates have been proposed.

The *Edda* is associated in its manuscript history with Iceland, but since Iceland was not settled until 870, it's probable that many of the poems were composed elsewhere and carried to the island on Viking ships. It is generally accepted that Snorri had access to the material it contains and drew on it for the *Prose Edda*.

THE KEY MANUSCRIPT

The most important manuscript of the *Poetic Edda* is called the Regius Codex. It was written in the late thirteenth century (probably around 1270). It was kept for many years in Copenhagen but now resides in Iceland. J.R.R. Tolkien was an expert on it and frequently lectured on it. His translation of part of it, *The Legend of Sigurd and Gudrún*, was published by HarperCollins in 2009.

Wherever it came from and whoever the author(s), the *Poetic Edda* has had an immense influence on the literature of Northern Europe. It contains the story of Sigurd and Brynhild, a Norwegian version of the German *Ring of the Nibelung*. It includes the *Völuspá*, the most important of the northern creation poems. In all, the Regius Codex contains twenty-nine poems or poetic fragments. (It possibly originally contained more; it is forty-five pages long but is missing eight additional pages.) In addition to this, most versions of the *Edda* add five more poems for a total of thirty-four.

The Völuspá

The *Völuspá* is a sustained account of the creation of the world and its peoples. Its name derives from the fact that the *völva*, or seeress, requests Odin if he would like her to tell of the formation of the world. With his assent, she proceeds to describe how the world was formed from the body of the giant Ymir (see Chapter 5). She recounts the creation of the first man and first woman and the struggle between the two races of gods, the Æsir and the Vanir.

THE DVERGATAL

In the midst of the *Völuspá* is a "catalog of dwarves," that is, a list of dwarf names. However, most scholars believe this was added to the poem later and was not part of the original. Among the names listed were:

- Durinn
- Náinn
- Bífurr
- Báfurr
- Bomburr
- Nóri
- Gandalfr

- Thráin
- Thorinn
- Fíli
- Kíli
- Dóri
- Óri

Readers of Tolkien's *The Hobbit* and *The Lord of the Rings* will, of course, recognize the source of many of the fantasy author's dwarf names.

As well, the seeress describes the killing of Baldr, most beautiful of the gods, through the treachery of Loki, and the subsequent efforts of Odin to bring his beloved Baldr back from Hel (see Chapter 7). Finally, the poem speaks of Ragnarök, the ending of the world, and the rebirth of a new world from the ashes of the old (see Chapter 14).

General scholarly consensus is that the *Völuspá* was written in the tenth century and was used as a source by Snorri, since he quotes from it extensively in parts of the *Prose Edda*. There was probably significant Christian influence, since this was a period when Scandinavia was transitioning from paganism to Christianity. Indeed, some have argued that the purpose of the poem was to preserve some version of the older religious traditions.

In order, the poems in the *Poetic Edda* are:

LAYS OF THE GODS

- *Völuspá.* The epic poem of the creation of the world.
- *Hávamál.* Verses attributed to Odin containing wisdom and advice.
- *Vafthrúdnismál.* A conversation between Odin and Frigg and later between the giant Vafthrúdnir about the structure of Norse cosmology.
- *Grímnismál.* A long catalog of proper names. Odin, in disguise, is being tortured by King Geirröth. Bound between two blazing fires, he speaks to the king's young son, Agnar.
- *Skírnismál.* The ballad of Skirnir, the messenger of Freyr; Skirnir is sent to Giant Land to aid Freyr in his wooing of the giantess Gerdr.
- *Harbardsljod.* An exchange of insults between Thor and Odin.
- *Hymiskvida.* A recounting of Thor's fishing contest with the giant Hymir and of his nearly successful attempt to catch the World Serpent.
- *Lokasenna.* This is Loki's taunt to the assembled gods of Asgard.
- *Thrymskvida. The Lay of Thrym*, this is the story of the theft of Thor's hammer and the comic episode in which Thor is disguised as Freyja to recover it.
- *Alvíssmál.* The dwarf Alvis wishes to marry Thor's daughter and is forced to endure a long interrogation by the god.
- *Baldrs Draumar.* Odin travels to Hel to learn why his son Baldr has been troubled in his sleep. Here Odin hears that Baldr will die at the hand of Hödr.

- *Rígsthula.* A poem about the origins of the world in which a god named Ríg creates the various classes of beings that inhabit the earth.
- *Hyndluljod.* The wise woman Hyndla is asked by Freyja for the genealogy of one of her favorites, Ottar. This leads to the genealogy of many of the heroes of Norse mythology.
- *Svipdagsmál.* The love story of Svipdag and Mengloth.

LAYS OF THE HEROES

- *Völundarkvida.* The story of an artisan, Völund, who is captured by a king, hamstrung, and forced to work on an island, making beautiful objects for the king. The story is parallel to that of Wayland the Smith, which was widespread in Germanic mythology.
- *Helgakvida Hjorvardssonar.* The story of Helgi, son of the Norse king Hjorvard.
- *Helgakvida Hundingsbana.* Another lay of Helgi. In this poem he is called the son of Sigmund and there is mention of Sinfjotli, the son of Sigmund and Signy.
- *Fra dauda Sinfjotla.* This poem gives more detail to the story of Sinfjotli, already told in the *Völsunga Saga*.
- *Grípisspá.* Young Sigurd has a conversation with his uncle, Grípir, in which the uncle foretells Sigurd's path through life.
- *Reginsmol.* An account of the conversation between the dwarf Andvari and Loki, when Loki takes the former's gold to put in an otter skin (see Chapter 11).
- *Fáfnismál.* The story of Fafnir, who becomes the dragon slain by Sigurd and thus the latter's source of glory as well as wealth.
- *Sigrdrífumal.* In these verses, which tell of the meeting of Sigurd

and Brynhild, the latter is identified with Sigrdrífa, who, because of her disobedience toward Odin, is imprisoned in a circle of fire.

- **Brot af Sigurdarkvidu.** The end fragment of a longer poem, *The Lay of Sigurd.*
- **Gudrúnarkvida I.** The first *Lay of Gudrun*, this forms a kind of coda to the *Saga of the Volsungs*, in which Gudrun, Sigurd's widow, tells of finding his body and then of her wandering for five years and her eventual remarriage to Atli.
- **Sigurdarkvida en Skamma.** An account of the conspiracy of the brothers against Sigurd and of his slaying.
- **Helreith Brynhildar.** After her death, as Brynhild travels the road toward Hel, she is accosted by a giantess, to whom she tells further details of her unhappy life.
- **Drap Niflunga.** Atli becomes Gudrun's second husband after the death of Sigurd, and she avenges her husband's murder by killing her brothers Gunnar and Hogni.
- **Gudrúnarkvida II.** The second part of *The Lay of Gudrun.*
- **Oddrúnargratr.** Oddrún, sister of Atli laments for her lost lover Gunnar.
- **Atlakvida en Grönlenzka.** A further telling of the story of Atli and of Gudrun's revenge for the death of Sigurd.
- **Atlamál en Grönlenzku.** Another poem dedicated to the deeds of Atli and the slaying of the sons of Gjúki.
- **Gudrunarhvot.** The story of Svanhild, daughter of Sigurd and Gudrun, and the wife of Ermanaric, king of the Goths, who after being falsely accused of adultery was trampled to death by horses on orders from the king.
- **Hamdismál.** The sons of Gudrun, Hamdir and Sörli, take revenge upon the Goths for the death of their sister.

SKALDIC POETRY

One further source of Viking myth is the works of skaldic poets. There is an overlap with the *Poetic Edda* here, since some of the skaldic poets wrote works that are preserved within it, while other compositions exist as separate poems. Generally, the term "skaldic" refers to those poets writing in the Scandinavian royal courts and Iceland during the Viking age and beyond. They used complicated forms of poetic diction; hence the need for Snorri's guide to poetic forms that is contained in the last part of the *Prose Edda*.

Snorri is numbered among the skalds; other important ones include:

- Eyvindr Finnsson (tenth century)
- Hallfredr Óttarsson (tenth century)
- Úlfr Uggason (tenth century)
- Thórarinn loftunga (eleventh century)
- King Harald Hardrada (eleventh century)

Chapter Five

IN THE
BEGINNING . . .

T his is how it was in the beginning.

Before the earth came into being, there were two realms: To the south lay Múspell, a world that was bright and hot. Flames rose from it hundreds of feet into the air. No being who was not from Múspell could dwell there for the fearful heat. At the very edge of the realm stands the Black One, Surtr, a fire giant. He bears a flaming sword and guards against all outsiders. On the day the world ends, he will battle against the gods, destroying them and the earth with a great fire from his blade.

In the north was the freezing realm of Niflheim. There were snows and eternal ice, and the air was itself frozen. From Niflheim eleven rivers came forth, all emerging from a great spring called Roaring Kettle (Hvergelmir). These rivers are:

- Svol
- Gunnthra
- Fjorm
- Fimbulthul
- Slid
- Hrid

- Sylg
- Ylg
- Vid
- Leiptr
- Gjol

This last river, Gjol, lies adjacent to the Gates of Hel, the dark underworld, and separates the souls of the living from those of the dead. All these rivers poured their flowing waters into the space between Niflheim and Múspell. This was called Ginnungagap, the Yawning Void. As the waters fell into Ginnungagap, they froze, and the ice gradually filled the void. Near the top, it was warmed by the fires of Múspell and transmuted into clay.

THE CREATION OF YMIR

From this ice-formed clay was shaped a giant, a man named Ymir. It is from him that all the race of giants comes.

YMIR THE EVIL ONE

During his visit to Asgard, Gylfi (disguised as Gangleri; see Chapter 4) asked the three Æsir if Ymir was a god. "No!" replied the Æsir named High. "In no way is he a god. He is the father of all frost giants, but he is evil and so the race of frost giants is evil."

In his sleep, rivulets of sweat came from Ymir's armpits. From that sweat of his left arm were formed the first man and woman. The sweat from his great legs merged and formed a son. These were first of the frost giants, enemies of the Æsir.

THE COW AUDHUMLA

Also from the clay that had given birth to Ymir there came a great cow, Audhumla, to give the giant nourishment. Her udder brought forth milk that the giant drank. To sustain herself, she began to lick the salty rime on Ginnungagap, and as she did so she licked the outline of a man. As Snorri tells us in the *Prose Edda*:

> She licked the blocks of ice, which were salty. As she licked these stones of icy rime on the first day, the hair of a man appeared in the blocks toward evening. On the second day came the man's head, and on the third day, the whole man.

The man was called Búri, and he was the father of Borr, who in turn would sire Odin by the woman named Bestla. Bestla was the daughter of a giant, so the greatest of the gods, Odin, has giant blood running through his veins.

Odin and his two brothers, Vili and Vé, now perceived that Ymir and his offspring were a danger to them. So they armed themselves well and fought with the giant. Their battle shook the worlds above and below until at last Ymir fell, pierced with many wounds.

Blood gushed from his wounds and it drowned the race of frost giants except for one, Bergelmir, and he fled together with his family and followers. They hid themselves from the wrath of Odin and gradually Bergelmir was able to restore the race of frost giants to plague the Æsir.

THE MAKING OF MIDDLE-EARTH

But as for the dead Ymir, the three brothers, Odin, Vili, and Vé, took his body and placed it in Ginnungagap. From his blood they made the sea, and they caused the sea to flow all around the land, surrounding it and binding it together. From his flesh they fashioned the earth, and they used his bones to make soaring mountain cliffs.

They raised the giant's skull above the earth and called it the sky, and at each of its four corners they placed a dwarf to support the sky. The dwarves were called North, South, East, and West. The sparks that shoot randomly from Múspell's fires they took and placed in the sky to light it.

THE STARS IN THEIR COURSES

Snorri, in the *Prose Edda*, quotes a poet to the effect that when the stars, sun, and moon were placed in the sky, they did not know their true courses, and it was some time before these were firmly established.

The Building of a Fortress

But the sons of Borr were not done yet. They gave the lands on the very edge of the earth, between the earth and the sundering sea, to the clans of giants to dwell in. Then, using the eyebrows of Ymir, they built a great wall around the rest of the earth and they called it Midgard (Middle-earth). They hurled the giant's brain into the sky, and it became the clouds.

Now the sons of Borr walked their earth and they came upon two trees, an ash and an elm. From the wood of these trees they made a man and a woman. Snorri says, "The first son gave them breath and life; the second, intelligence and movement; the third, form, speech, hearing, and sight." The man was called Ask, which means ash tree, and the woman was called Embla, or elm. These were the ancestors of the human race.

HOENIR AND LODUR

According to the *Völuspá*, which forms part of the *Poetic Edda*, Odin's companions on the occasion of the creation of man and woman were not Vili and Vé but two other brother gods, Hoenir and Lodur. Nothing more is known of these gods.

Asgard and the Æsir

In the middle of Midgard, the sons of Borr built a mighty fortress called Asgard. This is the home of the gods, where they carouse and from which they go out into Middle-earth to visit the race of men and, sometimes, to do battle against the giants.

Asgard was approachable only by a bridge called Bifrost, which, to humans, appeared as a rainbow.

The Æsir and the Vanir

Besides the Æsir, there was another race of gods, the Vanir. It included Freyr and his sister Freyja as well as their father, Njord. Njord conceived the children by his sister but is married to the disagreeable goddess Skathi. He lives at Noatun where he rules over the waves and weather and was therefore of particular importance to the Vikings.

ÆSIR AND VANIR

There has been a great deal of discussion among scholars of mythology about the existence of two groups of gods and thus two separate cults. Njord and the Vanir seem to have been more popular in Sweden, whereas Odin and the Æsir were popular in Norway, Denmark, and later Iceland. It has also been suggested that the gods of the Vanir were more associated with fertility than those of the Æsir.

War soon broke out between the two races of gods, the first war fought upon Middle-earth. Eventually the conflict ended in a truce. Njord, Freyr, and Freyja were sent to the Æsir as hostages, while the Vanir received the wise god Mímir.

VALHALLA AND THE VALKYRIE

In the midst of Asgard, the gods built a mighty hall, which they named Valhalla. Here gather half the heroes who fall in battle (the other half belong to the goddess Freyja). Before the doors of Valhalla stand the golden trees called Glasir, shedding their bright-shining red-gold leaves across the doorstep. These trees are the most beautiful of any trees in the world.

In Valhalla, the warriors are fed on pork that never gives out, and the udders of the goat Heidrun bring forth mead instead of milk. It is important that they be well fed, because these warriors will be the champions of Odin during Ragnarök. Thus it is a mistake to think that all warriors automatically go to Valhalla; it is a company of select fighters, chosen by Odin.

The historian Saxo Grammaticus quotes from a speech by a warrior, Biarki, to the following effect:

> War springs from the nobly born; famous pedigrees are the makers of War. For the perilous deeds which chiefs attempt are not to be done by the ventures of the common men. . . . No dim and lowly race, no low-born dead, no base souls are Pluto's prey, but he weaves the dooms of the mighty . . .

Thus the stories in Viking mythology are about the deeds of gods and men of noble lineage. Common folk rarely enter into these tales, and if they do it is merely as supporting players.

Each day, the heroes in Valhalla do battle with one another, but at day's end, the slain are brought back to life. So the cycle of battle, death, and rebirth goes on as it will for ceaseless years until the ending of the world comes with Ragnarök.

The Valkyrie

The warrior heroes are escorted to Valhalla by the Valkyries, maidens clad all in shining armor who decide who will live in battle and who will die. Brynhild is among the most famous of the Valkyries. They wait upon the heroes gathered on the mead benches of Valhalla, bearing them food and drink.

In some respects, as scholars have pointed out, the Valkyries are similar to the Norns in that they foretell men's fates. However, the Valkyries are specifically focused on battles. Their myth may reflect the fact that in some places Viking women fought in battles. Certainly there were priestesses who presided over the sacrifice of prisoners of war in the wake of a conflict. In the instance we mentioned earlier (see Chapter 1) of the sacrifice of a slave girl, the observer noted that the ceremony was led by a woman. The chronicler noted that she was "an old Hunnish woman, massive and grim to look upon."

OTHER RACES OF MIDDLE-EARTH

In addition to the gods, the giants, and humans, the world also included dwarves and elves. We have seen already that the sons of Borr made four dwarves to hold up the sky. Dwarves were earth-dwelling craftsmen. They could create marvelous treasures but were often reluctant to share them with others. They were squat and ugly, drinking great quantities of mead and keeping themselves to themselves. In some versions of the mythology, they grew from rotting maggots on Ymir's body.

The Mead of Poetry

Among the prizes of the dwarves was a magical mead, although they did not create it. The tale shows the treachery and untrustworthiness of the dwarven race.

It came about this way:

After the conclusion of the war between the Æsir and the Vanir, the gods spat into a great cauldron to seal their truce and guarantee the lives of the hostages. From their spittle, they created a man named Kvasir. He was the wisest of the Vanir, and he traveled here and there, answering questions and resolving disputes.

However, when he visited two dwarves, Fjalar and Galar, he did not perceive the blackness in their hearts. He did not see the treachery in their eyes or notice the evil on their brows. The two dwarves killed the wise Kvasir, and from his blood they brewed a wonderful mead. If anyone drank the mead, he became a poet and scholar, filled with the power of creation.

The Dwarves' Treachery

Nor was this the end of the dwarves' evil deeds. They befriended a giant named Gilling and persuaded him to come to sea with them in their boat. Once they were safely out of sight of land, they tipped the boat and cast Gilling into the water, leaving him to drown. They then returned to shore and informed his wife that her husband had died in an accident. They planned to take her to sea and drown her as well, but Galar grew tired of her lamentations and when she came out of her house, he dropped a millstone on her head and killed her as well.

But here the dwarves met their reckoning. For Gilling and his wife had a son, Suttungr, and when he heard of the death of his parents, he guessed the two dwarves were to blame. He seized them by the scruffs of their necks and dragged them into the water. Far from shore was a reef, and when he reached it, he deposited the dwarves on it. "It is too far to swim," he snarled at them. "So when the tide comes in and this reef is covered . . ."

"Wait!" cried Galar. "We have something for you." And he told Suttungr about the magic mead made from the blood of Kvasir. "It's yours if you let us off this rock and carry us back to shore."

Suttungr thought for a while, but at last he agreed. He carried the hapless dwarves to land, and they—with no other choice in the matter—gave him the cauldron of mead. Suttungr took it to his home and put his daughter, Gunnlöd, in charge of guarding it.

Odin's Theft

Despite Suttungr's efforts to keep the matter silent, word spread of the mead and its powers. Odin decided that as the most important of the gods, he must have some of it.

He disguised himself as a man named Bölverk and traveled to the home of Baugi, Suttungr's brother. Baugi greeted his guest and set to complaining about how hard times were. He had no workers to tend his crops, he said, because all his slaves had killed one another. (In truth, it was the disguised Odin who had persuaded them to kill one another in rivalry for Bölverk's amazing whetstone.) Bölverk expressed sympathy. "I am willing to do the work of your nine slaves," he said. "I ask only one thing in return: Give me a drink from that mead that your brother guards so jealously." Baugi agreed, and throughout that summer Bölverk labored on Baugi's farm. But not a drop of the mead would Suttungr yield to his brother or his worker.

In the face of Suttungr's intransigence, Bölverk/Odin proposed a trick to Baugi. He gave the farmer a drill. "Use this to drill a hole in the mountain where Gunnlöd guards the mead," he said.

Baugi balked a bit at deceiving his brother and his niece, but in the end he dug the hole. To his astonishment, his laborer was suddenly transformed into a snake and slipped down the hole into the heart of the mountain. Horrified, Baugi struck at him as he went down the hole but missed.

At the other end of the hole, Odin emerged and instantly changed into the shape of a handsome young man. He greeted the astonished

Gunnlöd, who was both impressed with his beauty and mindful of her father's injunction to guard the precious cauldron. But Odin used all his wiles until at last she yielded. "All right!" she cried. "If you sleep with me one night, I'll give you a single drink of the mead."

Odin smiled. "I'll sleep with you three nights, fair one, and take three drinks," he offered. The girl agreed, since she did not see how the young man could drink enough of the mead to make a difference.

So for three nights they slept together, and on the fourth day Odin arose and went to the cauldron.

His first drink drained it by a third. Then he took a deep breath and took another long swallow. Now the cauldron was more than two-thirds empty. As the horrified girl realized she had been tricked, Odin took a final draught and drained the cauldron empty.

Suttungr sprang into the cavern. A glance told him what had happened, and he rushed at the young man. But Odin put his arms by his sides. Feathers sprouted from him. He flapped his wings, and as an eagle he swooped out of the front door of the cavern and soared away.

Not to be outdone Suttungr changed to an eagle as well and leaped in pursuit. On the two flew, passing over the lands at such speed that to men below they seemed like a breath of wind. From afar, the Æsir in Asgard saw them coming. Quickly they put out containers, and Odin spat the magic mead into them. From thence forward, gods and men were gifted in poetry and wit because they imbibed the magic mead the dwarves had made from Kvasir's blood.

The Meaning of the Tale

The previous story is notable for several reasons. First, as we said earlier, it is an illustration of the treachery and evil character of dwarves in Viking myth. At the same time, the dwarves are consummate craftsmen and creators. It's notable that the Germanic word for a poet is *scop* (pronounced "shop"), which is related to the modern English verb *shape*. Thus a poet is one who shapes language in much the same way as a smith might shape iron, bronze, or gold.

Another point about the story is that Norse myths are fascinated by shape changing. We will find this coming up again and again, particularly in stories featuring Loki, the trickster who relies on deception for many of his deeds. But as we can see, Odin, chief of the gods, is not above practicing it.

The reasons for the prevalence of this device in northern myth are not clear. It may have something to do with the play of sunlight on water, which can make shapes seem fantastically variable. As a people who spent much time at sea, the Vikings were well aware that things are not always what they seem.

A third element in the story is the device of a man sleeping with a woman (or a woman sleeping with a man) in order to obtain a reward. We will come to this again later in the story of Freyja and the necklace of Brísingamen.

Elves

Elves of northern myth are not nearly so unpleasant as the dwarves, but they are also a more marginal part of the world. They remain largely unseen by other races, although beautiful elven maidens will sometimes attempt to seduce human men. It was customary for households to make a sacrifice to the elves at the beginning of the winter months.

There were two races of elves: the Light Elves were beautiful, fair as gods; the Dark Elves, on the other hand, were ugly and black-hearted. In some versions of the myths, the Dark Elves are indistinguishable from dwarves. For the most part, Dark Elves dwell underground, while Light Elves live on or near the surface of Middle-earth.

THE DARK ELVES OF D&D

Fans of Dungeons & Dragons, and in particular readers of the novels of R.A. Salvatore, may recognize characteristics of the Dark Elves of the Forgotten Realms. Salvatore's murderous race of dark elves live in their vast underground city of Menzoberranzan, engaged in intrigues that would put the Borgias to shame.

Some scholars argue that this dichotomy between a race of light, good elves and evil earth-dwelling elves persists in stories of fairies and goblins.

THE VIKING COSMOS

Like any mythology, the Vikings had many different versions of their cosmos. This is only natural, since until the twelfth century, most of it was not written down or systematized. (A dogmatized mythology is another term for religion.) Even Snorri Sturluson presented various competing ideas in his *Prose Edda*.

Nonetheless, we can get a fairly clear picture of what the Viking mythic world looked like. In all, there were nine worlds, arranged in three layers with three worlds in the first layer, four in the second, and two in the third.

Asgard and the Æsir

At the top is the world of Asgard, home of the Æsir, a land surrounded by a great wall. The land so enclosed is rich and fertile, as it should be to support a race of gods.

When the gods first began to build Asgard, there came a giant who was a great craftsman and offered to help them by building the encircling wall.

"What is your price for this?" Odin asked the giant.

"If I complete my labors in the space of a single winter," the giant replied, "you shall give me the fair Freyja to be my bride. And you shall also give me the sun and moon to be mine forever."

The gods laughed, for to build such a wall within the span of one winter seemed impossible to them. Odin readily agreed to the giant's proposal. "But," he said, "know this: If you fail in this task, your life is forfeit."

"Agreed!" replied the giant. Then he put fingers to his mouth and blew a long whistle. Up trotted a huge horse.

"What's this?" asked Odin.

"My horse, Svadilfari, who will help me build the wall."

As the gods watched, they saw that Svadilfari was of marvelous strength and size. All day and all night he helped the giant carry huge blocks of stone; indeed he did twice the work of his master. With only a few days before the onset of spring, the wall was almost finished. The gods were horrified that they might have to fulfill their end of the bargain; Freyja wept bitterly and reproached Odin for having agreed to give her in marriage to a giant.

Then Loki looked at them and smiled. "I have a plan," he said.

He changed himself into the likeness of a mare. Then he went to where Svadilfari was laboring and whinnied loud and long. Lust stirred in Svadilfari's loins. The stallion stopped in his work and trotted toward the mare. The master of disguise, Loki, wheeled and galloped away. After her galloped the stallion. The giant cursed in frustration, but he could not finish his work, and with a blow from his hammer Mjollnir, Thor crushed out his life. According to this account, Svadilfari caught up to the mare and impregnated her, and from the mare/Loki was born Sleipnir, Odin's eight-legged steed.

Alfheim and Vanaheim

As mentioned earlier, this level is also the site of Valhalla, where dead heroes go to await the end of the world, Ragnarök. In Valhalla, the heroes spend their time drinking (naturally) and fighting with one another, but at the end of each day the dead are revived to continue the battle. This may strike us as not much of a way to spend the afterlife, but it makes sense if we place it within the context of Viking life, which was largely filled with battles and raids and victory feasts.

The gods gather every day at the Well of Urdr, where they render judgments in the shade of the branches of Yggdrasil, the World Tree that stretches through all the nine worlds.

Also on this level are Vanaheim, home of the Vanir, and Alfheim, home of the Light Elves. It was remarked earlier that at the conclusion of the war between the Vanir and the Æsir, the two sides exchanged hostages: the Æsir got Njord and his children Freyr and Freyja, and the Vanir got Mímir, accounted the wisest of the Æsir.

The Vanir soon began to complain that they had had the worse of this bargain. In a rage, they drew their swords and axes and hacked off Mímir's head. Spitefully, they sent it back to the Æsir. But the latter had the advantage of them. Odin took the head, anointed it with herbs and oils, and gave it the power of speech. So ever after, Odin had the benefit of Mímir's wise advice.

Midgard, Nidavellir, Svartalfheim, Jötunheim

The second layer of the cosmos contained Midgard, otherwise known as Middle-earth. Midgard was surrounded by a sea that, as Snorri tells us, was so vast that "to cross it would strike most men as impossible." In this sea, lay the World Serpent, Jörmungandr, who surrounds Middle-earth; he is so huge that he bites his own tail.

OUROBOROS

A serpent devouring its tail is a very old mythological symbol and so common that it has its own term—ouroboros. Examples of this motif can be found in such divergent mythologies as those of Egypt, India, and China.

Outside the walls that surround Midgard lies Nidavellir, called the Dark Home. It is also sometimes called Svartalfheim, though in other versions this is a separate place below Nidavellir; in either case, it is the home of the Dark Elves. The dwarves live in this place as well. Author Kevin Crossley-Holland argues, "No valid distinction . . . can be drawn between the dwarfs and the dark elves; they appear to have been interchangeable." However, others disagree.

Finally, on this level we find Jötunheim, realm of the giants. It was dominated by the vast fortress of Utgard, a place where Loki and Thor had an engaging, if embarrassing, encounter (see Chapter 8). Since Utgard means "the outer world," it is not clear if it was situated on the far side of the impassable sea, although the adventure of Thor and Loki suggests it was not.

Jötunheim had a number of different subsections or territories. Among them were Thrymheim, where dwelt the giant Thiazi, who at one point forced Loki to help him capture the woman Idunn and her magic apples (see Chapter 10).

Niflheim, Hel

Niflheim is the world of the dead and is described as nine days' ride from Midgard. Hel is also a place of the dead, and the distinction between the two worlds is sometimes lost. Hel is described by Snorri as a gloomy spot, with towering walls and a great gate over which there presides a monster, both white and black, also named Hel. We are also indebted to Snorri for an account of one of the Æsir who went down to Hel to retrieve a beloved god.

Holding the whole structure of the cosmos together is the World Tree Yggdrasil, whose roots reach into each of the three levels. We will discuss this tree much more extensively in the following chapter. For now, suffice it to say that it both nourishes the worlds of the Viking cosmos and is constantly attacked by creatures from them.

This, then, is the setting for the Vikings' tales of daring, of magic, of treachery, death, and rebirth.

Chapter Six

YGGDRASIL, THE WORLD TREE

Running through all the nine worlds, linking them together, are the trunk and branches of a vast tree: Yggdrasil. Snorri, in the *Prose Edda*, describes this as the "central or holy place of the gods."

Yggdrasil is an ash tree, "the largest and best of all trees," to again quote Snorri. The tree has three roots:

- One reaches to the Well of Urdr (Urdarbrunnr)
- A second is among the frost giants at the former site of Ginnungagap
- A third reaches down to Niflheim

THE WELL OF URDR

The Well into which extends one of the three roots of Yggdrasil stands in the heavens, where there are many places of great beauty. Under the root of the World Tree there is a vast hall, and in it dwell three lovely maidens: Urdr (Fate), Verdandi (Becoming), and Skuld (Obligation). They are known as the Norns, and they decide every man's fate.

THE FATES

The notion of three women who decide each man's and woman's fate is found in Classical mythology as well. In Greek myth they were Clotho, the spinner; Lachesis, the allotter; and Atropos, unturnable. Clotho spun the thread of each man's fate, Lachesis measured the length of thread allotted to each, and Atropos chose where to cut the thread, assigning each person the means and manner of his or her death.

There are more norns, some descended from the elves and some from the dwarves.

In the *Prose Edda*, when Gangleri heard of this, he remarked, "It seems the norns are unfair in their allocations, since some people lead rewarding lives while others have little fame or wealth." The High explains to him, "The good norns, those who are well born, shape a good life. When someone has a bad life, it is the bad norns who are responsible."

Also at the Well of Urdr, the gods have their judgment place. Each day, they ride their horses across the bridge Bifrost, also called Asbru, or Bridge of the Æsir. It takes the form of a rainbow, and the High explains to Gylfi in the *Prose Edda* that the red seen in the rainbow is flames that guard the bridge from the giants.

Besides Odin's eight-legged horse, Sleipnir, the gods' steeds include:

- Glad
- Gyllir
- Glaer
- Skeidbrimmer
- Silfrtopp
- Sinir
- Gils
- Falhofnir
- Gulltopp
- Lettfeti

All the Æsir ride their horses to Urdr except for Thor, who wades the rivers to the site of the well.

HVERGELMIR

The root of Yggdrasil that reaches down into Niflheim ends at Hvergelmir, Old Norse for "Bubbling Stream." In *Grímnismál*, one of the poems in the *Poetic Edda*, it is identified as the source of all waters in the nine worlds and the place where liquid from the horns of Eikthyrnir, a stag that resides on the top of Valhalla, falls:

> Eikthyrnir the hart is called,
> that stands o'er Odin's hall,
> and bits from Lærad's branches;
> from his horns fall
> drops into Hvergelmir,
> whence all waters rise.

Thus all waters in the nine worlds begin in the dark depths of Niflheim.

THE CREATURES OF THE TREE

The World Tree is no passive support for the nine worlds. It is their central spire and is tormented by various creatures that traverse it or gnaw on it.

Nidhogg

Chief among these creatures is Nidhogg, a dragon forever chewing on the root of the World Tree far below in Niflheim. As well, Nidhogg chews the souls of men who have been sent to Náströnd, a place in Hel where those guilty of murder, adultery, or breaking their oaths are condemned to remain forever. In Náströnd, as well as the torments administered by Nidhogg, the condemned are subject to torture by snakes and the bites of the wolf Fenriswolf.

THE NAME YGGDRASIL

There is considerable dispute among scholars over the meaning of the name Yggdrasil. The consensus is that in Old Norse it means Odin's Gallows, but it's not clear why it should have this name. It may possibly relate to the myth that Odin hung from the tree for nine nights to attain the secret of runes (see Chapter 7).

The Harts

In addition to Nidhogg's attacks on its root in Niflheim, four harts dwell in the branches of Yggdrasil, where they devour its leaves. Their names are Dáinn, Dvalinn, Duneyrr, and Durathrór. In the poem

Grímnismál, part of the *Poetic Edda*, Odin describes the agony that Yggdrasil feels.

> Yggdrasil's ash   great evil suffers
> Far more than men do know;
> The hart bites its top,   its trunk is rotting,
> And Nidhogg gnaws beneath.

Ratatoskr

At the very top of Valhalla there is an eagle, and in between its eyes sits a hawk. All the night and day, the squirrel Ratatoskr runs between the eagle and Nidhogg carrying messages from the birds, stimulating the dragon to fury. Some scholars have interpreted references in the *Poetic Edda* to mean that the squirrel also gnaws on Yggdrasil.

On the other hand, the tree has some relief, for the three Norns splash water on its root so it will never wither and die. Snorri says:

> That water is so sacred that all thing which come into the spring become as white as the membrane called *skjall* which lies on the inside of an eggshell . . .
>
> People call the dew, which falls to the earth, honey dew and bees feed on it. Two birds nourish themselves in the Well of Urd. These are called swans, and from them comes the species of bird with that name.

SVIPDAG AND MENGLOTH

The World Tree figures in a romantic myth about two young people destined for one another but seemingly separated by an impassable gulf. Here is how it came about.

Svipdag was the son of Groa, a seeress who dwelt in dark Niflheim. But his father had married an evil woman who tormented her stepson. She told him that the only woman he could marry was Mengloth. This was as good as telling him that he could not marry at all, since all men knew that Mengloth dwelt far off in a fortress guarded by many magical beasts.

In despair, he sought advice and assistance from his mother. He braved the darkness and steam and smoke of Niflheim and called upon her. When at last she came forth, he told her of his woes.

"I will cast nine spells upon you," she said. "They will aid you on your road and prevent others from hindering you on it. Let none turn you aside."

So Svipdag set out, traveling the length and breadth of the nine worlds, searching for Mengloth. At last in Jötunheim, land of the giants, he encountered a great fortress ringed by flame. At the gate stood a giant.

"Who are you?" asked Svipdag.

"Who are you?" snarled the giant. He hefted his club.

"Just a traveler," replied Svipdag cautiously. "What is your name?"

"Fjolsvid. You'd best go back the way you came. There is nothing for you here. What did you say your name was?"

"Vindkald, son of Varkald, son of Fjolkald. Who is master of this great hall?"

"No master but a mistress, Mengloth of Many Necklaces."

Now Svipdag began to question Fjolsvid about the hall's defenses. "Tell me," he said, "what is that gate?"

"It's called Thrymgjol and if you touch the latch it will trap you."

"What is the name of this fortress that is so mighty that it dwarfs the hall of the gods?"

"It is called Gastropnir, which means That Which Crushes Guests. I built it from the clay of the giant Leirbrimir. It will last while the world lasts."

"What is the great tree that spreads its branches across the sky?"

"That is Yggdrasil, the World Tree. Its roots reach down to Asgard and Niflheim, but no man has seen all its roots. It will not fall by axe or by fire."

At last, Svipdag asked, "Tell me, Fjolsvid, who is the man who can hope to win the fair Mengloth?"

"Only one man," replied the giant. "Svipdag, for he and he alone has been chosen as her husband."

"Rejoice!" cried Svipdag. "For I indeed am he! Bear this news to Mengloth that she may draw back her defenses and greet her one true love."

The giant went to his mistress. "Lady Mengloth," he said, "you had better come to the gate. There is a man there who claims to be the chosen one for you. The dogs bend down before him, and the gate has opened before him."

Mengloth was suspicious. "If you are not telling me the truth," she said, "endless will be the torments visited upon you." She arrayed herself with the help of her maidens and went to the fortress gate.

"Who are you?" she said. "What do your kinsmen call you? If I am to be your bride, I must be sure you are the right man who has been chosen by fate for me."

"My name is Svipdag, son of Solbjart. I have crossed the world for you, and now I have found you."

Mengloth opened her arms. "Svipdag!" she cried. "My love! I have long waited for you."

As they embraced, she said, "I have so longed for this day!"

"My love," he replied, "I too have longed with you. But from now on, we will never be parted."

Grógaldr *and* Fjölsvinnsmál

The story of Svipdag and Mengloth is told in two poems of the *Poetic Edda*, *Grógaldr* and *Fjölsvinnsmál*. The first tells the story of Svipdag's appeal to his mother and the nine charms she casts on him, while the second contains the account of Svipdag's interrogation of the giant Fjolsvid. The number nine was significant in Viking mythology and recurs in a number of places (there are, of course, nine worlds in the Viking cosmology).

At some point—probably around the seventeenth century—the two poems were conflated into a single poetic work, the *Svipdagsmál*. In tone it has a somewhat Arthurian ring; the hero goes on a long quest and must overcome obstacles along the way to find that which he seeks. In the end, though, true love wins through.

Chapter Seven

GODS AND GODDESSES OF THE NORTH

L ike the gods of the Greeks and Romans, the northern deities often showed an all-too-human side. They were jealous, spiteful, quarrelsome, and occasionally less powerful than some they encountered. They were strongly associated with natural forces and were appealed to by the Vikings for protection from those forces.

ODIN THE ONE-EYED

Chief of the gods was Odin. We owe a great deal of our knowledge about him and the other Viking gods to Snorri Sturluson's *Prose Edda*. Among the questions the disguised Gylfi asks the three figures he interrogates in Asgard is, "Who is the highest or oldest of the gods?"

The three inform him that this is the Allfather and has many other names, including Spear-Shaker (Biflindi), Fulfiller of Desire (Oski), and Ruler of Weather (Vidrir). This is Odin, and the three mysterious figures tell Gylfi/Gangleri his part in the making of the world.

Odin the Allfather

According to the three, there are twelve gods, and Odin is called the Allfather because he is their father. He is sometimes called the Father of the Slain, because those who fall in battle are his adopted sons. With these fallen heroes, he sits in Valhalla and another hall called Vingólf. As well, he is sometimes called the God of the Hanged, the God of Prisoners, and the God of Cargoes.

He has a magical spear, Gungnir, which will always hit its target (see Chapter 8). His eight-legged horse, Sleipnir, can outrun any other steed on earth. On his shoulders sit two ravens, Huginn and Muninn, that is, Thought and Memory. Each day they go out into the world and see all that goes forward and report back to their master. Odin said of them, "I fear to lose them, but most I fear to lose Muninn."

Odin himself spends much time sitting on the high rock of Hlidskjalf, where he can see and survey all of the nine worlds. Sometimes, though, he amuses himself by wandering through Midgard, disguised as an old man wearing a broad-brimmed hat.

Odin has only one eye, having sacrificed the other to obtain a drink from the Well of Knowledge. To gain the Mead of Poetry, he disguised himself as a serpent and wriggled his way into the midst of a mountain. And to gain the secret of runes, he hung from the World Tree, Yggdrasil, for nine days and nights.

The Secret of Runes

Runes were used by the Vikings as a magical writing. Since they were made up of straight lines, they could easily be chiseled into substances such as stone or bone.

Odin is credited with bringing the knowledge of runes to mankind. But to learn them, he had to undergo an ordeal, described in the poem called *Hávamál*. He hung, for nine days and nights, from Yggdrasil, first having gashed his side with a spear.

> I know that I hung
> On the windswept tree
> For nine whole nights
> Pierced by the spear
> And given to Odin
> Myself to myself.
> On that tree
> Whose roots
> No one knows
> They gave me no bread
> Nor drink from the horn
> I peered into the depths
> I grasped the runes
> Screaming I grasped them
> And then fell back.

Since this is the only allusion we have to the incident, it is hard to know exactly what to make of it. The implication seems to be that Odin hung above Hel, where the secret of the runes was kept, until at last he understood it. Yet at the same time, there is the implication of a sacrifice *to himself*. He suffers, much as a prisoner of war might; according to the chronicler Adam of Bremen, prisoners of war were sacrificed by the

Vikings as late as the eleventh century. Note that the sacrifices to Odin were generally performed by hanging the victim.

HEROIC SACRIFICE

The notion of the hero hanging from a tree to gain knowledge or to sacrifice himself is common to northern mythology and extends into the Christian era. In the Anglo-Saxon poem "The Dream of the Rood," the story of the crucifixion is told from the point of view of the cross, which in the poem can be seen as parallel to Yggdrasil. The cross sees Jesus coming toward it:

> I saw then the Savior of mankind
> hasten with great zeal as if he wanted to climb up on me . . .
> He stripped himself then, young hero—that was God almighty—
> strong and resolute; he ascended on the high gallows,
> brave in the sight of many, when he wanted to ransom mankind

A far different image than the usual view of the crucifixion, but one more fitted to a warrior society.

The word "rune" comes from the Danish *run*, meaning "mystery." So the runes were involved in mysterious—that is to say, magical—knowledge. Historian Tony Allan in his book on the Vikings argues, "It seems likely that runes played an essential part in the ritual sacrifices of the Viking era—since they had to be reddened with blood to be effective—and they were also used to cast lots for divination."

Runes might be carved in objects to give them special meaning; a whalebone with a runic inscription might be used to invoke the favor of the gods during childbirth or before a battle. In *Egil's Saga*, the hero finds a young girl who has fallen ill. In her bed, Egil finds a bone with runes carved on it. Then he says:

> No man should carve runes
> unless he can read them well;
> many a man goes astray
> around those dark letters.
> On the whalebone I saw
> ten secret letters carved,
> from them the linden tree
> took her long harm.

Egil cuts some new runes and places them beneath the girl, who promptly feels much better.

Odin and Billing's Daughter

Odin was married to Frigg, but as with so many gods in so many cultures, that marriage rested on a shaky foundation. Odin had an eye for a pretty woman. As he learned to his cost once, though, it is unwise to trust such a woman.

In his survey of the nine worlds, Odin beheld Billing's daughter sleeping in Midgard. She was, he later said, the most beautiful woman he had ever seen, and he thought that the world would become a desert and perish if he could not sleep with her. But when he came to her, she was cautious.

"Not until after dark," she said to the Allfather. "No one must discover we are lovers."

In his lust, Odin agreed to wait, hard though it was. The minutes crept by like hours and the hours seemed like days. But when he came to her chamber at midnight, something was wrong. The warriors in the place were all awake, and the hall was lit by torches.

The father of the gods retreated. At dawn he returned, and now the warriors were asleep on their mead benches. But of the maiden, there was no sign. And to her bed, as a gesture of contempt for Odin, she had chained a bitch.

And so, as Odin was wont to say afterward, no woman is to be trusted until she has been put to the test.

LOKI

Depending on one's reading of the source material, Loki was not a god but a mortal who, nonetheless, spent most of his time with the gods. Snorri says (more precisely, High tells Gangleri) that Loki has many names. Among them are Slanderer of the Gods, Source of Deceit, and Disgrace of All Gods and Men. According to the *Prose Edda* he is the son of the frost giant Farbauti and his mother is Nal or Laufry. With Angrboda (Sorrow Bringer) he had three children: Fenriswolf, Jörmungandr, and Hel.

Fenriswolf

The first of these children was Fenriswolf, sometimes called Fenris (or Fenrir) and Hrodvitnir. When Odin learned of the birth of these children of Loki and Angrboda, he knew of the great sorrow they might bring to Midgard. And he knew of his own danger, for it had been prophesied that at Ragnarök, the ending of the world, Fenriswolf should be the death of Odin. So he sent the Æsir to gather the children together and bring them to Odin so the Allfather might bind them.

The Æsir struggled to take Fenriswolf. Ever they approached him, and ever he snapped at them with his great jaws. The Æsir made a great chain and called it Læding. It was strong enough, they felt, to bind the wolf.

The beast allowed them to wind it about his limbs. Then he inhaled and strained, and with little effort on his part the chain links burst asunder, and Læding lay in ruins.

The Æsir made another chain, stronger than Læding; it was called Dromi. They showed it to Fenriswolf. He thought it strong, and again he allowed the Æsir to wind it about him. Then he shook and strained and pulled, and Dromi broke, just as Læding had done.

Now the gods sent to Svartalfheim, the realm of the Dark Elves. And the Dark Elves agreed, for a payment of gold, to make a new chain that could not be broken by any power in the nine worlds.

The Æsir approached Fenriswolf for a third time and showed him the new chain, named Gleipnir. Its links shone in the light, and it seemed to have no more than the thickness of a silk ribbon. But this time the wolf refused them permission to wind it about his legs. "It may be stronger than it looked," he growled knowingly.

"If you can break this chain," said one of the Æsir, "we will cease our attempts to bind you, and you will be free to go where you wish."

THE WOLF OF NARNIA

C.S. Lewis was a friend of J.R.R. Tolkien. Like Tolkien he was an enthusiast of Norse mythology. While his friend was writing *The Hobbit* and other tales of Middle-earth, Lewis wrote a series of young adult novels set in the magical land of Narnia. In one of these, *The Lion, the Witch, and the Wardrobe*, a terrible white witch rules the land, which is in a state of perpetual winter—"always winter and never Christmas" as one of the characters says sadly. The witch's chief assistant is a wolf named Fenris Ulf, who serves as the chief of her secret police. The wolf is killed toward the end of the novel by the heroic boy Peter, who later becomes High King of Narnia.

Fenriswolf could not resist this offer. He allowed the ribbon of iron to be woven about him. "But," he said suddenly, "as a token of your good faith, one of you must place his hand in my mouth. The Æsir looked at one another. Then Tyr spoke up.

"I will do it," he said, and he placed his hand in the wolf's mouth.

Now Fenriswolf swelled and drew breath into his lungs. He strained against the chain. Sweat appeared on his brow, and he strained again. Gleipnir trembled and creaked, but it did not break. A third time the wolf strained. A snarl came from the back of his throat. His jaws clamped down. Tyr gave a cry of anguish and pulled back his arm, but it was too late. The wolf had bitten off his hand.

Now the Æsir took another chain called Gelgja and fastened one end to Gleipnir. The other end they bound to a great rock called Gjoll. They put that rock a mile below the surface of the earth and placed another vast rock on top of it. Fenriswolf snarled and slavered.

Now one of the Æsir drew a sword and drove it through the wolf's jaw from below into the roof of his mouth. The wolf shrieked with agony, for now it was gagged and bound. Saliva ran from his mouth in such amounts that it formed a river called Von, or the River of Spit.

And there Fenriswolf waits for Ragnarök and the end of time.

Jörmungandr

The second of Loki's terrible children was Jörmungandr, the great serpent. Odin saw its growing size and terror and he caused it to be placed around Midgard at the bottom of the sea that surrounds Middle-earth. The serpent grew so vast that it itself surrounded Midgard and put its tail into its own mouth.

Once Thor, strongest of the gods, succeeded in lifting it (see Chapter 8), although it was disguised as a cat so he did not know what feat he had performed. And once Thor, on a fishing trip (see Chapter 9) caught the serpent and lifted its head where he could see it. However, as he prepared to kill it with his hammer, his companion cut the fishing line and freed the serpent. Like Fenriswolf, Jörmungandr will remain in his place until the end of the world.

Hel

The third child of Loki was Hel. She was assigned by Odin dominion over Niflheim and the realm of the dead (there is a significant distinction in that warriors who die in battle go to Valhalla, whereas men, women, and children who die of other causes go to Hel).

In art, Hel is almost always depicted as an old woman, haggard and dressed in tattered robes. The gates to her realm are guarded by her hound Garm. Her hall is called Eljudnir, and it is to there that the god Hermódr travels to beg for the return of the god Baldr, slain through the treachery of Loki (see Chapter 10). She has a dish called Hunger, a knife called Famine, a slave named Lazy, and her servant is called Slothful. (All of this is according to the *Prose Edda*; there is no other description of Eljudnir and its inhabitants in any other source.)

THE HAG

The image of a hag is extremely common in mythology. The Celts had the Morrígan, a figure foretelling death in battle. As well as Hel, Scandinavian folklore spoke of the *mara*, the figure of a withered old woman who perched on the chests of sleepers and gave them nightmares.

The Trickster

Loki himself plays a major role in Viking mythology, and it is usually not a very good one. He exists, it seems, to twit the other gods and to play practical jokes on them, but in some cases, such as the death of Baldr, these jokes go very wrong. He is wed to Sigyn, who in the end must aid him when he is bound by the gods for his treachery (see Chapter 10).

In the *Lokasenna*, part of the *Poetic Edda*, Loki is on full display. Much of the poem consists of a long string of taunts aimed at the gods (insults seem to have been an important part of Viking culture).

Ægir, god of the sea, also called Gymir, has prepared a feast for the gods after having obtained the cauldron from the giant Hymir (see Chapter 9). Among those who come to the feast is Loki, who speaks to Ægir's serving man Eldir and asks him who is within the hall. When Eldir tells him, Loki replies:

> In shall I go
> into Ægir's hall,
> For the feat I fain would see;
> Bale and hatred
> I bring to the gods,
> And their mead with venom I mix.

Once within the hall, he proceeded to spew forth insults. It is worthwhile to quote his exchange with Bragi, which is typical of his conversation:

> Hail to you, gods!
> ye goddesses, hail!
> Hail to the holy throng!
> Save for the god
> who yonder sits,
> Bragi there on the bench.

To which Bragi replied:

> A horse and a sword
> from my hoard will I give,
> And a ring gives Bragi to boot,
> That hatred thou makest not
> among the gods;
> So rouse not the great ones to wrath.

Sneering, Loki replies:

> In horses and rings
> thou shalt never be rich,
> Bragi, but both shalt thou lack;
> Of the gods and elves
> here together met
> Least brave in battle art thou,
> (And shyest thou art of the shot.)

Bragi answers:

> Now were I without
> as I am within,
> And here is Ægir's hall,
> Thine head would I bear
> in mine hands away,
> And pay thee the price of thy lies.

Finally, Loki replies:

> In thy seat art thou bold,
> not so are thy deeds,
> Bragi, adorner of benches!
> Go out and fight

> if angered thou feelest,
> No hero such forethought has.

The exchange is interesting, not only for what it tells about Loki's sense of humor and his habit of spreading discord among the Æsir but also because it is the sort of rough banter and quarreling that was likely all too common among the Vikings and other inhabitants of Scandinavia. In a male-dominated society where feasting was accompanied by testosterone-fueled arguments, it is surprising that more arguments did not end in bloodshed.

OTHER GODS

Snorri mentions a number of other gods, though none as important as the three major deities: Odin, Thor, and Loki. Those he lists include:

Baldr

Baldr, as we shall see later, is a tragic figure in Viking mythology (see Chapter 10). Snorri mentions him early in the *Prose Edda* as the second of Odin's sons. He is beautiful, so much so that a light shines forth from him. He is also the wisest of the gods, the most well spoken, and the most merciful. However, a consequence of the latter quality is that he is prone to indecisiveness. His hall is in a place called Breidablik.

Njord

Njord has already been mentioned as among the Vanir. He is the ruler of the seas, and his home is at Noatun, which means Enclosure for Ships. Sailors and fishermen offer sacrifices to him, so he was a particularly important god as far as the Vikings were concerned.

Freyr

Freyr is a member of the Vanir. Along with his sister Freyja and his father Njord, he was sent to Asgard as a hostage in the wake of the war between the Æsir and the Vanir (see Chapter 7). He is a fertility god and is also associated with sacral kingship (the notion that the king has both religious and temporal functions and significance), virility, and prosperity. This makes him one of the most important of the northern gods.

He weds the giantess Gerdr (a fact that further illustrates the complex relations between the giants and the gods), but in doing so he must give up his sword. He is, however, possessed of other magic treasures: the ship Skidbladnir, which can hold all the gods when at sea but can be folded up to no larger than a piece of parchment when on land; and the boar Gullinbursti, which is made of gold and will run about the land, uncaught by any man or god, and shines with a brilliant light from its bristles.

Because Freyr lacks his sword, he is destined to be killed by the giant Surtr during the events of Ragnarök.

Tyr

Tyr was referred to previously in the story of the binding of Fenriswolf. Because of the loss of his hand, he is often warlike in his disposition, but he is also courageous and very wise.

Bragi

Bragi is particularly well spoken and eloquent in the art of poetry. One can perhaps see why Loki should have impugned Bragi's courage, since he is not among the warlike of the Æsir. He is married to Idunn, who keeps the magical apples that forever preserve the youth of the gods (see Chapter 10 for the tale of Loki's theft of the apples of Idunn).

Heimdall

Heimdall is sometimes called the Gold Toothed, since his teeth are made of gold. He was born of nine maidens; Snorri calls him "powerful and sacred." He lives near Bifrost, the rainbow bridge from Midgard to Asgard, and with his telescope he keeps track of the mountain giants to ward off any attempt they may make to cross the bridge. He sees things up to 100 leagues off and hears the grass growing and sheep's wool rustling. If there is an assault on Asgard, he will blow his horn, Gjallarhorn, to rouse the Æsir.

More Viking Deities

Here are the names of some of the other Viking gods:

- **Ægir.** The king of the sea, akin to Classical mythology's Triton. In the *Skáldskaparmál*, Snorri identifies him with the sea giant Hiér.
- **Hödr.** He is blind but very strong, and memory of his works will long endure among men and gods.
- **Vídarr.** He is the silent god. He has a shoe of immense thickness that he will use at Ragnarök to kill Fenriswolf. Only Thor exceeds him in strength.
- **Vali.** Also known as Ali, he is the son of Odin and Rind. He is skilled in battle and has a keen eye.
- **Ull.** He is the son of Sif and thus the stepson of Thor. He is skilled with the bow and with skis and is a fine warrior. Snorri says he is the best god to pray to in the event that the suppliant is involved in single combat.
- **Forseti.** He is the son of Baldr and Nanna and is skilled before all the gods at rendered justice. In his hall called Glitnir, he hears legal cases and adjudicates them fairly.

GODDESSES

Viking society, and Scandinavian society generally, was male-centric; thus goddesses do not play nearly as prominent a role in the mythology of the north as they do in, say, Celtic or Classical myth. Nonetheless, there are several important ones.

Frigg

Of all the goddesses, Frigg has primacy. She is the wife of Odin and has great power in her own right.

DAYS OF THE WEEK

Among the most lasting legacies of Norse myth are the names of the days of the week. Some are named for Greek or Roman gods—Saturday, for example, is named for Saturn—but others are names for gods of the north. Wednesday takes its name from Wotan, the German version of Odin; Thursday is, of course, Thor's Day; and Friday is the day belonging to Frigg.

Frigg is the mother of Baldr, and his death is a great grief to her. Later, when she hears that Odin will die in Ragnarök, this becomes her second great grief. The parentage of the Æsir is somewhat confusing and contradictory. According to some sources, Thor is the son of Frigg and Odin, while other sources give him other antecedents.

Frigg's hall is Fensalir (derived from the word for "wetlands"). She has considerable power of foreknowledge, but this often brings her sorrow.

Freyja

Freyja is the goddess of beauty; she is also associated with fertility, gold, and war. She rides in a chariot drawn by cats and weeps tears of gold. Like her brother Freyr, she is of the Vanir rather than the Æsir. She receives half of those who die in battle (the other half belong to Odin) and receives them in her hall, Sessrúmnir. She is married to Ódr but because of his absence, she weeps tears of red gold for him.

ÓDR OR ODIN?

Some scholars argue that in fact Ódr is simply Odin by another name, although this seems to contradict the idea that Odin is married to Frigg, something that is widely supported in the source material.

Freyja, like her counterpart in Classical myth, Aphrodite, is often vain and capricious. Both qualities are on display in the tale of her acquisition of the necklace of the Brísings (see Chapter 9). Nonetheless, because of her connection to fertility, worship of her was widespread. Many plants in the north bore her name, although as often as not they were renamed with the coming of Christianity. To a degree, early Christians among the northern peoples may have identified her with the Virgin Mary.

Other Goddesses

Snorri, in the *Gylfaginning*, names a number of other goddesses with brief descriptions of them. They include:

- **Soka.** She lives in a hall at Sokkvabekk.
- **Eir.** She is described by Snorri as "the best of doctors."

- **Gefjun.** She is a virgin, and women who die as virgins are said to serve her.
- **Fulla.** She is a handmaiden of Frigg and carries about the goddess's accouterments in an ash box. She also looks after Frigg's footwear.
- **Sjofn.** She is concerned with love, and lovers pray to her, as well as to Freyja. Snorri says that the word for "lover," *sjafni*, comes from her name.
- **Lofn.** She is a sweet, loving goddess. On account of her gentle goodness, Odin has given her permission to arrange unions between men and women even if these have been forbidden by men.
- **Var.** She listens to the contracts and agreements made between men and takes vengeance upon those who break their oaths.
- **Vor.** She is careful and knowledgeable, and nothing can be hidden from her. The word "aware" (*vor*) comes from her name.
- **Syn.** She is the guardian against those who ought not to enter a hall. She also defends legal cases that the prosecution should not win.
- **Hlin.** Those whom Frigg wishes to be protected from danger are watched over by this goddess.
- **Snotra.** She is wise and courteous and gives her name to a man or woman who is wise (*snort*).
- **Gna**. She is Frigg's messenger, traveling throughout the nine worlds on her horse Hofvarpnir, which can ride on sea and on land.

These, then, are the northern gods and goddesses, worshipped by the Vikings and many others until the coming of Christianity.

Chapter Eight

THE EXPLOITS OF THOR

L oki was sly and not particularly strong—he relied for his triumphs on his craftiness and his ability as a shape-shifter. Thor, on the other hand, was a mass of brawn that left relatively little room for brains. After Odin, he was perhaps the most widely venerated of the Norse gods. This is hardly surprising among a people known for their prowess in battle. Thor is described as huge and red bearded with a great thundering voice (indeed, Thor was occasionally referred to as the Thunderer).

THOR'S ORIGINS

Snorri Sturluson, in the *Poetic Edda*, claims that Thor was descended from the line of the kings of the city of Troy. According to Snorri, King

Priam's daughter Troan married a man named Mennon, and they had a son whom they named "Tror, the one we call Thor."

TROJAN ORIGIN STORIES

By the time Snorri was writing in the thirteenth century, many European peoples had origin myths that connected to Troy. The British, for example, were said by the twelfth-century author Geoffrey of Monmouth to be descended from Brutus, a prince of Troy. The most famous of these origin stories was contained in the Roman Virgil's poem the *Aeneid*; Virgil, writing in the first century B.C.E., had claimed that the Romans were descendants of Aeneas of Troy.

By the time Thor was twelve years old, Snorri says, he had reached his full strength, demonstrated by the fact that he could lift ten bear skins in a pile. He traveled widely, killing giants, warriors, and a fierce dragon.

In another account, Thor is the son of Odin and the goddess Jord, which means "Earth." He married a prophetess named Sif, and they live in a 540-room mansion, the largest building ever constructed. He traveled in a chariot drawn by two magical goats, Tooth-gnasher and Tooth-gritter. These goats had magical properties, as we shall see shortly.

Widespread Popularity

Thor was the thunder god—as his chariot passed through the sky, the Vikings said, it made the noise of thunder. He was the god of travelers, which may account for the fact that his cult spread throughout all the lands traversed by the Vikings. Of the population of Iceland, 25 percent had names that in some way featured the name "Thor." When the Icelandic parliament, Althing, met, he was considered to be present. There are numerous depictions of him, and in almost all of them he can be identified by his most important weapon: his hammer.

THOR'S HAMMER, MJOLLNIR

As with many Viking myths, the story of how Thor obtained his great hammer begins with a joke of Loki's. Sif, Thor's wife, was among the most beautiful of the goddesses; she was particularly noteworthy for her shining golden hair, which glowed with a light all its own. One night as she and Thor lay sleeping side by side in their bed, Loki entered the room. With a sweep of his knife, he sheared off Sif's golden hair, leaving it in pile on the floor.

Sif was desolate when she awoke and saw what the Trickster had done. Thor raged at Loki, who cried that it was merely a joke. "I will replace it," he whined. "I will get help from the dwarves!"

Loki sought out two dwarves and persuaded them to make Sif a new head of hair, this one made of real gold. In return, he promised them the friendship and goodwill of the gods of Asgard. Grudgingly, the dwarves agreed and built a blaze beneath their forge. Using its heat, they fashioned strand after strand of shining gold. Soon, they had a great mass of golden hair, which rustled and fluttered when the dwarves blew on it.

But the two dwarves did not stop there. Wishing to cement their friendship with the gods, they fashioned two other marvelous items—a spear for Odin and a ship for Freyr.

The spear was called Gungnir and would never miss whatever target at which Odin hurled it. The ship, which was called Skidbladnir, was large enough to hold all the gods but it could be taken apart and stored in a size no bigger than a piece of cloth.

The Other Dwarves

Loki thanked the brothers, but he did not go straight back to Asgard. Instead, he turned aside to the dwelling of two more dwarves: Brokk and Eitri. These dwarves were fascinated by the treasures Loki bore, but they boasted that they could outdo them.

The Trickster sneered at their claim, but the dwarves kindled their own fire at their own forge and began work. Eitri soon produced a statue of a boar with bristles of gold. Then the dwarves created an arm ring, also of gold. Finally, they brought forth a hammer of iron with a short handle and a massive head. The two dwarves told Loki to take the treasures back to Asgard and let the gods decide which were greater. But if their treasures were deemed superior, Brokk would claim Loki's head as a reward.

The gods were overwhelmed by the treasures (and Sif was very glad to get her hair back). The dwarves told Odin that the arm ring, called Draupnir, was for him. "Every ninth night," they said, "eight rings of similar weight and value will fall from him." To Thor, they said, "The hammer is Mjollnir. No matter where you hurl it, it will always come back to you, and if you want to hide it, it will become small." Then they asked the gods what was the most valuable of the six treasures laid before them.

The gods were of one mind: Mjollnir, because with it, they knew, Thor could defeat their mortal enemy the giants and keep the walls of Asgard safe.

Loki's Defeat

Since the gods had chosen one of the treasures he and his brother had wrought, Brokk laid claim to Loki's head. Thinking fast, the Trickster told the dwarf, "Very well, but the head only. Don't take any part—even the slightest—of my neck." (Students of Shakespeare's *The Merchant of Venice* will recognize this trick, which in the play is used by Portia to save Antonio from the evil Shylock.) Recognizing that he'd been tricked, Brokk angrily declared that he would sew Loki's lips shut and proceeded to do so with the aid of his brother's awl. Although Loki tore out the stitches, he howled in pain.

THOR AND LOKI'S JOURNEY TO UTGARD

One of the central myths that Snorri Sturluson recounts in the *Poetic Edda* is the story of a journey that Thor and Loki made to Utgard, a dwelling place of giants. At this time, there was not war between the giants and Asgard. The two gods traveled in Thor's chariot, drawn by the goats Tooth-gnasher and Tooth-gritter. Toward evening, they came to the house of a farmer and his family. The gods asked for shelter, and while the farmer was happy to provide it, he warned them that he had no food to give them.

"No matter," replied Thor. He took his goats and slaughtered them, while the farmer's family looked on, astonished that he would casually destroy the beasts that drew his chariot. The farmer's wife cooked the goat meat, and then Thor invited the family to feast. But, he warned, they should throw the bones onto the goatskins, which he spread before the fire.

The family fell upon the meal heartily, since they were very hungry. As they had been bade, they threw the bones onto the skins. But when the god's back was turned, the father, who was still hungry, took one of the leg bones and cracked it with his knife so he could suck out the marrow. Then the family and the gods lay down by the fire and went to sleep.

The next morning, Thor consecrated the goatskins with his hammer. Behold, the goats stood up again, as alive as ever. But as they walked toward the chariot, Thor noticed that one of the goats was limping. Turning on the farmer, he roared, "Who has done this thing? Who has broken my goat's thighbone?" Trembling, the farmer confessed what he had done.

Thor lifted his hammer above his head, and the farmer, in terror, pleaded, "Please don't kill me! Take anything else! Take my family!"

Thor's rages, like summer lightning storms, were spectacular but never lasted long. Lowering his hammer, he growled, "Very well. Your children will accompany us as servants." Thus the boy, Thjalfi, and the girl, Roskva, went forward with Loki and Thor and, according to Snorri, remained Thor's bonded servants ever since.

Thor and Skrymir

When darkness overtook the four travelers, they searched for a place to rest. They found a hall with a long passageway and a door at the end of it. Grateful for the shelter, they lay down, but in the night they were woken by a great earthquake. The hall shook and trembled, and even Thor and Loki were startled by the suddenness of the earth's movements.

In the morning, Thor went out to explore, taking with him the belt of strength, which enabled his divine power to make him larger. He beheld a great man sleeping, whose snoring was fit to wake the gods themselves. When he awoke, Thor asked his name, and the man replied it was Skrymir. He recognized Thor and greeted him respectfully. However, Thor does not appear to have returned the favor. He was more shocked when the great man showed him his glove, and Thor realized that this was what he and his companions had been sleeping in the night before. The glove's thumb was the hall in which they'd slept.

"Let's pool our provisions," Skrymir suggested, "and tonight we'll both feast well." Thor agreed, and the two piled their food into a common sack. All day they walked, Thor and Loki and their companions trailing after the tirelessly striding giant. When they finally stopped for the night, Thor was ravaged with hunger. "Come," Skrymir said. "Untie the bag and take what you want," and he lay down and went to sleep. Thor picked up the bag, thinking that he and his companions would have a hearty feast. But try as he might, the god could not undo the bag. His anger grew with his frustration, and he took his hammer, Mjollnir, and struck the giant in the head. Skrymir turned over and opened one eye at the god. "I think a leaf from a tree fell on my forehead," he told the god. "You should bed down and take your sleep."

Crestfallen, Thor agreed and fell into a fast sleep.

At midnight, the giant raised the forest with his snoring; the trees shook, and animals fled the sound. Thor woke and, angered again, he lifted his hammer, and this time he struck Skrymir at the middle of his skull. But although the hammer sank deep into the head of the giant, Skrymir awoke again and said, "Has an acorn, perhaps, fallen upon my head?" He brushed his head, clearing it of the invisible missile, and went back to sleep.

Thor was now torn between fury, hunger, and sleep. He trembled with the thought that his hammer might have found something it could not slay. As the red sun rose over the horizon, he also rose and rushed forward, crying in anger, and struck the sleeping giant on the temple with his hammer. This time the hammer sank deep, and the god was sure he had slain the sleeping giant.

Skrymir shrugged and stretched. "Come, friend!" he said. "It's time to get dressed. It seemed to me that some birds were cheeping above me and dropped some leaves and twigs upon me." Sullenly, Thor dressed and prepared to resume his journey.

Thor and Loki were on their way to Giant Land, to the stronghold of Utgarda-Loki. Skrymir gave them some advice: "The followers of Utgarda-Loki are very mighty. They won't tolerate bragging from some tiny fellow such as yourself. My suggestion is that you turn back now while you still have all your limbs. Still, I suppose you intend to continue. Folks such as you usually do. My path, though, leads northward to the distant mountains." So saying, he picked up his mighty food sack and stepped on his way. "In this parting," recounts Snorri Sturluson, "there is no report that the Æsir mentioned they were looking forward to meeting him again."

Arriving at Utgard

The next day the companions reached a great fortress. It was so large that they had to bend their necks all the way back to look up at it. It was far greater than anything that could have been built by the hand of man. Clearly, this was the stronghold of Utgarda-Loki.

They tried to open the door but could not budge it. Finally, they squeezed through the bars and found themselves in a great hall in which many folk, all of them giants, were sitting. At the far end of the hall, a great giant was sitting in a wooden chair. Slowly they paced the hall and, arriving before the giant leader, hailed him as Utgarda-Loki.

However, he ignored them at first. Finally he said, grinning contemptuously, "Am I right that this little fellow who I see before me is the famous Thor? The god of whom so many great deeds are spoken? There must be more to you than meets the eye! But all who stay in this hall with us must show they have primacy in some skill or other. What skill are you unsurpassed in?"

Thor was silent, but Loki spoke up. "I have the skill of eating," he said. "I can devour the meat that lies on this table"—he gestured to the great table at which the giants were seated—"faster than any of you."

Utgarda stared at him hard. "That would be an accomplishment indeed!" he said. He called to one of the giants, a being called Logi, which means "fire." Logi and Loki seated themselves at opposite ends of the table, and when Utgarda gave the signal, they began to eat. Loki reached the middle of the table, having eaten all the meat that was on his half. But Logi had eaten not only the meat but also the bones and the table itself.

Utgarda grunted. "It seems Loki has lost that contest," he observed. He pointed to Thjalfi. "What can that youngster do?"

Thjalfi had long, clean limbs. He said he would run a race against any Utgarda might name. The giant called a small fellow whom he named Hugi. The company went outdoors, where there was a broad plain. Thjalfi and Hugi crouched in their positions and when Utgarda cried the word, they ran swiftly. But Hugi ran so fast that when Thjalfi reached the end of the race, Hugi was already standing there waiting for him.

In the second race, Thjalfi fell even farther behind his opponent; at the end, he trailed by the distance of a long bow shot. And in the third race, by the time Hugi had reached the end, the panting Thjalfi was not even at the halfway mark.

"The lad has lost," declared Utgarda. He turned to Thor. "Now we come to you, god of Asgard. There are many tales of your deeds. What skill do you propose to show us?"

"Drinking!" replied Thor.

"Well spoke!" declared Utgarda. He commanded his cupbearer to bring Thor the horn from which his followers usually drank at their feasts. "There is only one condition," he said to Thor. "This horn is best if it is drunk in a single draught."

Thor had every confidence in his ability to do this. He lifted the horn to his lips and, as he thought, drained it. But when he lowered it, he could see that the level of drink was not much lower than before.

"Now," said Utgarda, "this surprises me. I would have thought that the mighty Thor could have drunk much more than that. But maybe you'll do better on a second try."

Thor drew a deep breath and drank again. This time, as he drank, he noticed he could not hold up the bottom of the cup as high as he would like. Nonetheless, he was confident he had drained the horn. But when he set it down, he saw that again the level of liquid had diminished only slightly.

Utgarda shook his head. "If that's the best you can do," he said, "you will not be considered as great a man among us as you are by your compatriots at Asgard. Come! Try one more time."

For a third time, Thor drank. For a third time, he swallowed until he felt as if he would burst. And for a third time he set the horn down on the table. But within it, the drink was still there, almost as if he had not tasted it.

Utgarda's Cat

Now Utgarda said, "Perhaps there's something besides drinking you're better at. What about a feat of strength?" Thor nodded assent, for he was particularly proud of his strength, which was unmatched among the gods. Utgarda smiled. "This test will be very simple," he said. "All you must do is lift my cat."

A gray cat strolled into the hall and sidled up to Thor. The god bent down to pick her up. But as he lifted his hand, the cat arched her back. The farther Thor brought up his hand, the more the cat arched until her back was high above his head. Finally, Thor lifted and stretched, and this time one of the gray cat's paws lifted from the ground. But that was all.

Utgarda said, with laughter in his voice, "Well, that went as I expected. After all, my cat is large and Thor is only a little fellow."

The Wrestling Match

Thor was furious. "Let someone wrestle with me!" he shouted. "Then you will see whether or not I am little!"

Utgarda motioned to the crowd of giants, and an old hag came forward. She was bent with age, and her name was Elli. Thor grappled with her, but to his astonishment, she proved more than a match for him. Time and again, he struggled to throw her, and time and again she held her ground. Finally, the Thunder God himself was forced to one knee.

"That is enough!" said Utgarda. "There is no need of more contests." And he showed Thor and his companions to their sleeping places.

The Explanation

Early the next morning, the travelers made ready to depart. Utgarda accompanied them through the great gates and out onto the plain. There he stopped them and spoke as follows:

"Now I will tell you the truth about your visit, for I am the one who will decide if you are ever to be admitted to Utgard again. I was Skrymir, whom you met in the forest, and I deceived you with shape changing. I fastened our food bag with wires so that even with your great strength you could not undo it. When you struck me with your hammer, you might have done me great damage or even killed me, but with my magic I turned your blows aside. But they did not go unmarked. See that flat-topped mountain with three square valleys in it, one deeper than the others? Those are the marks of your mighty hammer.

"When Loki offered to outeat one of my giants, I summoned Logi, who is wildfire itself. There was no way Loki, fast at eating though he is, can outeat a wildfire, which destroys everything in its path.

"Hugi, whom Thjalfi raced against, was in reality my thought. And no one can be expected to outrun my thought.

"And you, Thor, you could not compete against me either. When you drank from the horn, you did not realize that its other end was attached to the sea. No one can drain the sea dry. But when you come to the ocean you will see how much you have lowered it, and your draughts are now known as the tides. When you tried to lift my cat and succeeded in lifting one of its paws from the ground, all in my court were amazed. For in truth, the cat was no cat but was the Midgard serpent, which encircles all the world, biting its own tail. And you succeeded in moving it.

"When you wrestled with the crone, you were unaware that she is old age, which no one—not even the mightiest warrior—can defeat.

"Do not come again. I will use more trickery to defeat you."

In a rage, Thor lifted his hammer to destroy Utgarda. But the giant was gone. Thor turned back, intending to lay flat the mighty stronghold in which he and his companions had spent the night. But all that was to be seen was a broad, flat plain.

Chapter Nine

MORE TALES OF THE GODS

One feature of Viking myths that recurs over and over again is shape changing. Perhaps this is a consequence of so many days and nights spent on the ocean, where the sparkling sun and water can lead to mirages and a sense of unreality about what one sees. The gods, particularly Loki, are adept at changing their forms, from animals to birds, to humans. In the previous chapter we saw that the giant Utgarda was able to deceive Thor and Loki with his shape-shifting. The following story is told by Snorri Sturluson as part of the *Prose Edda*.

THOR AND HYMIR FISHING

After his humiliation at the hands of Utgarda, Thor was not long back at Asgard before he decided to make another expedition to the lands of the giants. He disguised himself as a young boy and set off one morning without companions. He made his way to the home of the giant called Hymir. When morning came, the giant rose to go fishing. Thor, in his guise as a boy, begged to be allowed to accompany the giant and offered to row back. The giant was dismissive. "You're nothing more than a boy," he growled. "Where I go and as long as I stay out . . . you'll freeze to death!"

Thor was angered by the giant's condescension and almost cast off his disguise so he could let his hammer slam into the giant's head. But he caught himself in time.

"If you take me with you," he said in his boy appearance, "I won't affect at all how far you row out. And we'll see which of us wants to come back first!"

The giant grunted and told Thor he'd have to supply his own bait. The god found some oxen belonging to Hymir and ripped off the head of one. "Now I have bait," he told the giant.

They started rowing, and Hymir said that was enough; this was where he fished. "I want to go farther," said Thor.

They rowed farther and farther, and Hymir said they were in danger because of the Midgard serpent. "No matter," said Thor and kept on rowing.

At last they stopped, and Thor baited his hook with the oxen head. He cast it into the deep. Snorri tells us:

> And it can be said in truth that this time Thor tricked the Midgard Serpent no less than Utgarda-Loki had tricked Thor into lifting the Midgard Serpent with his arm.

The Midgard Serpent opened its mouth and swallowed the ox head. The hook dug into the gums of its mouth, and when the serpent felt this, he snapped back so hard that both of Thor's fists slammed against the gunwale.

Thor was furious and used his divine strength so that both his feet pushed through the bottom of the boat. With his feet on the floor of the sea he began pulling the serpent onboard what was left of the boat. Thor stared straight into the terrible eyes of the beast that encircled the world, while Hymir grew pale, and sweat dripped from his brow.

Thor caught up his hammer and lifted it. Light from the rising sun gleamed from it. But just at that moment Hymir seized his knife and slashed the line so the serpent went free. Even as it sank into the waves, Thor hurled his hammer at it, and some say the hammer struck the serpent's head off. Then Thor punched Hymir so hard behind the ear that the giant fell out of the boat. And Thor, now grown to his true size, waded back to shore, leaving the giant and the wreckage of the boat behind him. Thus was Thor revenged upon the giants for his humiliation in the stronghold of Utgarda-Loki.

Hymir, Thor, and Jörmungandr

The story of Thor's fishing expedition exists in several versions. Snorri Sturluson includes it in the *Prose Edda*, and it is the subject of *The Lay of Hymir*, one of the poems collected in the *Poetic Edda*. Thor and the World Serpent, Jörmungandr, are enemies and will have their final battle in Ragnarök, the end of the world. As we saw earlier, Thor succeeded in lifting the serpent while at Utgarda (albeit unwittingly).

In *The Lay of Hymir*, the Æsir visit Hymir because they hear he is in possession of a marvelous cauldron, "a league deep," which can hold enough mead for all the Æsir at once. Thor eats so much food that he and Hymir must go fishing together, which leads to Thor's attempt to catch Jörmungandr and Hymir's thwarting of the attempt.

THE NECKLACE OF BRÍSINGAMEN

One evening in the middle of the night, the goddess Freyja left her hall, Sessrúmnir. She was unmarked in her departure by any save Loki, who followed after her. On and on she went, past a frozen river, across a glacier, over barren plains dotted with great boulders. At last she came to a narrow pathway that led down. She followed it, and Loki followed behind, unseen by her.

The pathway led to the forge of four dwarves: Alfrigg, Dwalin, Grerr, and Berling. The goddess stopped, amazed by the beautiful objects that lay scattered across the cavern. Among them one stood out—a necklace made of gold, its intricate strands twisted in a complex pattern that dazzled the eye and stirred the soul. Her heart was filled with desire for the thing.

She cast aside her cloak, and the dwarves too were consumed with desire, but theirs was for the beautiful goddess.

"I want the necklace," she told them. "I will give you whatever you wish if you will gift it to me."

The four dwarves conferred with one another and then, smirking, turned back to her. "There is only one thing we desire," their leader said. "The favors of the goddess Freyja, most beautiful of all the Æsir."

Freyja's heart was filled for loathing for the dwarves, but it was also overflowing with lust for the necklace. "Very well," she assented.

Loki saw all that went on.

For four days and nights Freyja slept with each of the dwarves in turn. At the end of her ordeal, the necklace was fastened about her slender neck, and she passed out of the cavern and returned to her hall.

However, Loki had gone before her, and he stood before Odin and told the one-eyed god of Freyja's treachery. Then he taunted Odin, saying that the god must be truly blind, and not merely in one eye, for such a thing to have occurred. "Where was your vision, O High One?" he sneered. "Do you not have the two ravens, Huginn and Muninn, who bring you news of all that happens in the world? Were you asleep when they told you of Freyja and her shameless conduct with the dwarves?"

Odin bellowed in anger at Loki. "Bring me the necklace!" he demanded. "Too often you have set us gods against one another. Now I charge you: Bring me the necklace!"

Loki, in fear, agreed to do as Odin wished.

The Trickster approached Freyja's hall, but it was locked. He changed himself into a fly and circled the hall, searching for a way to enter it. At last he found a tiny opening and squeezed his way through it. Freyja was asleep, still wearing the necklace.

Loki transformed into a flea and bit the goddess so that she tossed and turned in her bed until at last the clasp of the necklace was exposed. Then, assuming his own shape, Loki softly stole the necklace and fled from the hall.

When the goddess awoke, she reached for the necklace and realized it was gone. Raging, she went to Odin, whom she was sure was behind the theft. "Give me my necklace!" she demanded.

Scowling, the one-eyed god rebuked her for her conduct with the four dwarves. There was, he told her, only one thing she could do to regain the necklace for which she had sold her body. "Bring war to Midgard," he told her. "Set two kingdoms against one another!" And then he added, "But bring life back to the corpses of the fallen, so that each day, as the sun sets, the dead rise and do battle again on the morrow."

So great was her lust for the necklace, called Brísingamen, that Freyja agreed.

THE WEIRD OF BRÍSINGAMEN

In 1960, English author Alan Garner completed the children's novel *The Weirdstone of Brisingamen*. Although he borrowed the word "Brisingamen" (Brísingamen) from Norse mythology, the story itself has nothing to do with Scandinavia. Rather, it is a fantasy about two children caught in a conflict with dark magical forces. The book became the first in a series of critically acclaimed novels. Throughout them, Garner uses a mixture of terms borrowed from Scandinavian and Celtic myths, although with far different meanings than they originally had.

The Brísings

The origins of the term *Brísingamen* are unknown. The necklace is mentioned in the poem *Húsdrápa* by the poet Úlfr Uggason, who lived in the tenth century. A later account is given in the *Sorla Thattr*, which is part of a larger collection of tales, the *Flateyjarbók*, compiled at the beginning of the fifteenth century.

In some accounts, it's suggested that rather than a necklace it was a girdle. However, the scholar H.R. Ellis Davidson in *Gods and Myths of Northern Europe* argues that the suffix *–men* is used to indicate jewelry worn around the neck.

Snorri Sturluson says that Freyja owned the necklace, information he may have had from the *Húsdrápa*.

As to the meaning of "Brísings," that remains unclear. It's possible that they were a northern people. On the other hand, the word *brísingr* in Old Norse means "fire." Freyja's necklace thus seems to have been fiery, shining like a flame.

That Freyja should have been willing to sleep with four ugly dwarves to get the necklace is unsurprising, since she was known among the gods for her promiscuity. Loki claimed that she also took all the gods and the elves as lovers, although this may have been him trying to stir up trouble as usual. The Trickster even went so far as to say that she had had incestuous relations with Freyr, her brother. When the Vikings found themselves in trouble during a love affair, they were known to call upon Freyja for assistance.

The last part of the story is significant in that Freyja receives half of the warriors who fall in battle; the other half belong to Odin. The notion that she must revive warriors who fall and make them re-fight the battle is probably connected to this belief, but the storytellers do not explain precisely how.

HRUNGNIR AND THOR

Odin the Allseeing had a mind to visit the giants. So he mounted his eight-legged horse, Sleipnir, and galloped across the hills and valleys until he came to the dwelling of a giant name Hrungnir. Then Odin, in reply to a question from the giant about who he was, began to boast. "There is no equal of my brave steed!" he cried.

Hrungnir replied, "In this you are mistaken, for I myself have a horse, named Gullfaxi, that can take greater strides than Sleipnir, and his name means 'Golden Mane.'"

Contemptuously Odin wheeled his horse about and raced back the way he had come. But Hrungnir, anxious to pay the god back for his boasting, leaped on Gullfaxi and galloped after him. The two shot across the land like falling stars. Fast as Gullfaxi was, the horse could not overcome Odin's eight-legged steed. But so speedily was Hrungnir riding that before he realized it he had passed into the gates of Asgard.

Now the gods gathered around him and since he demanded drink, they brought him Thor's drinking bowls. To their astonishment, the giant drained the bowls, but he became very drunk and began again to boast.

"I will take Valhalla with me and carry it off to Giant Land," he roared. "I will destroy Asgard and slay all you Æsir! Save you"—he turned to Freyja and Sif—"you I will bring back with me to my hall."

Now there was thunder without Asgard, and Thor entered the hall in a rage. "What is *he* doing here?" he demanded. "Why have you invited him to drink among us Æsir? And why is Freyja serving him, as if he were one of us?"

Hrungnir stared angrily at Thor. "If I had thought to bring my weapons with me," he said, "we would even now be dueling at the place called Grjotunagardar, or the Courtyards of Rocky Fields. But I am here at Odin's invitation, and you would not be so dishonorable as to attack an unarmed man."

Thor was intrigued by the idea of a duel, since no one had ever challenged him to one. So the giant rose, went from the hall, and on his swift steed returned to his home. When the other giants heard of the duel, they realized that if Hrungnir could not win against Thor, there was no hope any of them could do better.

At Grjotunagardar the giants built a man of clay. He was nine leagues tall and three leagues wide, and his head was of stone. He had a shield of stone as well, and he stood next to the giant awaiting the coming of Thor. The Thunder God himself was stricken with fear when he saw the clay man, and he wet himself in terror.

The Death of Hrungnir

As the giant stood next to the clay man holding a huge whetstone as he waited for the Thunderer to attack, a young lad, Thjalfi, Thor's manservant, approached him and said, "Thor is burrowing beneath the earth and will come up beneath you. Stand on your shield if you want to prevent this."

Hrungnir did so, but then he saw thunder and lightning and knew the lad had lied to him. Then, a long way off, he saw Thor running toward him. The Thunder God raised his hammer, Mjollnir, and hurled it at the giant.

He in turn threw his whetstone, and it met Thor's hammer squarely. The whetstone broke in two, and one part fell to earth, and from it spring all whetstones. The other part of the whetstone struck Thor's head and laid him out. But the god's hammer struck Hrungnir in the head and crushed his skull. He fell, and his leg fell across the supine Thor, pinning him. Thjalfi tried to move the dead giant's leg but could not. All the other Æsir tried to move it, but none could budge it.

Finally, Magni came up to them. He was Thor's son by Jarnsaxa the giantess, and he was only three years old, but he cast aside the leg easily and told his father, "Alas I wasn't here or I would have defeated the giant by hitting him a blow with my fist."

Thor sat up and greeted his son warmly and as a reward gave him Hrungnir's steed Gullfaxi, though Odin said it was wrong to give the horse to the son of a giantess.

The whetstone remained in Thor's head. Once a prophetess named Groa made a magic to loosen it. When the whetstone began to move, Thor was happy, for he believed it would soon be out of his head. So he told Groa a story about how he had rescued her husband, Aurvandil the Bold, from Giant Land when Aurvandil was a baby. And Thor added that Aurvandil would soon return to her. At this, Groa became so happy that she forgot her magic, and the whetstone remained lodged in Thor's head. It is said that if anyone throws a whetstone across the floor, the stone in Thor's head moves, and the god groans with pain.

Sources for the Story

This tale is told by Snorri Sturluson in the section of the *Prose Edda* called the *Skáldskaparmál*. Among the tales contained in the *Skáldskaparmál* is the story of Sigurd the Volsung, which we'll take up in a later chapter.

The story reminds us that fighting and conflict are at the heart of Viking mythology. In the account of Valhalla, recall, the heroes gathered there spend all their time dueling, so it's easy to see why Thor jumps at the chance for a duel with Hrungnir. The story also brings to mind the Æsir's back-and-forth relationship with the giants; in this instance, Hrungnir is initially welcomed to Asgard as Odin's guest and, as he tells Thor, he is under Odin's protection.

THE GOLEM

The giant clay man fashioned by the giants to be Hrungnir's companion during the duel with Thor reminds us of the golem in Jewish mythology. The golem is a being created of mud or clay and magically brought to life. In the Talmud's version of the creation of man, Adam was created as a golem and brought to life by God.

THE *RÍGSTHULA*

The god Ríg was traveling along the shore of Midgard, gazing at the waters that stretched to the horizon and listening to the sounds of wind and wave. As night approached, he came to the farm of a couple named Ái and Edda. He knocked on the door of their cottage and asked for a meal and a bed. Grudgingly, they agreed and served him a scanty meal, poorly cooked. That night he slept between them. Nine months later, Edda gave birth to a son. The boy's skin was dark, and he was strong but ugly to look upon. Ái and Edda named him Thrael, which means "servant." He grew up and married a woman named Thír, which means "slave girl." The two had twelve sons and nine daughters, who became the race of thralls, serving others in Midgard.

The Second Night

On the second night of his journey, Ríg came to another farm where dwelt Afi and Amma. Again he requested food and shelter. This time the meal they gave him was good, and they were cheerful. The fire was warm and the bed was soft. Ríg slept between the husband and wife and in the morning went on his way. In nine months Amma gave birth to a boy whom they named Karl, or "freeman." When Karl grew up, he married a girl named Snör, which means "daughter-in-law." Karl and Snör had twelve sons and ten daughters, who were the ancestors of free farmers, craftsmen, and laborers.

The Third Night

On the third day of his journey, as Ríg continued along the shores of Midgard he came to a great house, a mansion. There he asked for food and shelter. The inhabitants of the mansion, Fadir and Módir, served him a splendid meal. The wine glowed ruby red, and the meat was savory and well cooked on the fire. Nine months later, Módir gave birth to a boy named Jarl, or "lord," whose hair was blond and whose face was beautiful. When Jarl was old enough to learn manly arts, Ríg reappeared at the mansion gates.

"The boy is my son," he declared, and he took Jarl away with him. Ríg taught Jarl many things, including how to read runes and how to fight. Jarl married Erna, daughter of Hersir. They had twelve sons but no daughters. The sons became the ancestors of noble warriors.

Chapter Ten

THE TREACHERY
OF LOKI

Tom Hiddleston notwithstanding, Loki is probably the most dislikable of the Viking gods. He is mercurial, violent, untrustworthy, a practical joker with a very cruel side to his humor, and, as we shall see in this chapter, someone whose jokes occasionally go very wrong indeed.

Loki is the foil to the gods' sense of self-importance. He is constantly tormenting them, bringing them to a better understanding of their own limitations. While most of the gods' actions in other myths rest on a firm understanding of their character and motives, Loki is often perverse. When he steals the hair of Freyja, it is not with any thought of gain but merely because he wants to do it. There is something childlike is many of his actions. In the myths recounted in this chapter we shall see his malice in both its innocent—and often comic—form and with the most tragic consequences.

THE THEFT OF THOR'S HAMMER

One day Thor awoke and, as was his custom, reached for his hammer, Mjollnir. But the hammer was not there. The Thunderer shrieked and swore, but his hammer was gone.

Thor turned for assistance to Loki, for who should better know of sly conduct and thievery than he? Loki turned to Freyja. "Will you lend me your falcon skin to search for Thor's hammer?" he asked.

"Were it made from gold," cried the goddess, "I would lend it to you." For she, and all the other Æsir and Vanir, knew that Thor's hammer protected them from the incursion of the giants.

Loki donned the guise of a falcon and he flew swiftly until he came to the land of the giants. He swooped down upon the court of Thrym, a king among the giants. "Have you stolen Mjollnir?" he asked, assuming his own shape.

Thrym laughed. "Truly things have gone badly among the gods," he sneered. "Yes, I have your precious Mjollnir! Eight miles underground I have buried it. And you will never get it back unless you pay my price."

"What is that price?" asked Loki steadily. Even then he was thinking how he could trick the giant into returning the precious hammer.

"My price is Freyja," replied the giant ruler. "If she will consent to be my bride, I will return Mjollnir to Thor."

Loki bowed his head. "This word will I return to Asgard," he said. And he became a falcon once more and leaped on the back of the wind. Swiftly he rode until he had returned to the abode of the gods.

"Well?" said Thor. "Have you found Mjollnir?"

"Yes," replied Loki. "It is in the hands of the giants. And they will only return it if Freyja consents to be the bride of Thrym.

All the gods cried out and were wroth with this news, but Loki the Trickster had an idea. "Wait!" he said. "Come, Thor."

"What do you mean to do," asked the Thunderer suspiciously, for he knew Loki of old.

"Freyja will not go to Thrym as his bride," replied Loki. "You will!"

Now all the gods of Asgard shouted in laughter—except for Thor. Heimdall said, "Let us drape the necklace of Brísingamen around his neck." And another said, "Let us array him as any bride would be, with a bunch of keys at his waist."

So each contributed their thought, laughing, and they took the Thunderer and swaddled him in a bridal gown and clasped the necklace of the Brísings around his neck and bound a bunch of keys at his waist.

"Who will you be," growled Thor to Loki.

"I will be your maidservant," said Loki calmly. "Come. Let us depart."

So Loki and Thor harnessed Thor's goats and rode forth to Jötunheim.

Now Thrym was moved to a frenzy and cried, "She is coming. Spread straw for her. Make ready the bedchamber!"

When Thor arrived, Thrym welcomed him and ushered him to the table in the hall, where a great feast had been prepared. "Sit you here," he said, "and all that you wish shall be placed before you."

Now, Thor felt hungry after his long journey. "An ox!" he cried. And so an entire ox was placed before him. Thor, in his disguise as Freyja, wolfed down the ox and Thrym looked on, astonished. "More!" cried Thor/Freyja. And so all the delicacies reserved for women were brought to him, and these too he ate. Then, to the astonishment of Thrym and the other giants gathered there, he drank down three horns of mead.

"Who has seen a bride with such hunger and thirst?" muttered Thrym to a giant sitting near him. He leaned toward his bride and lifted her veil. But Thor's eyes were not soft and doe-gentle like those of Freyja. "Her eyes are like burning coals!" shouted Thrym, drawing back.

Loki leaned in and said softly, "Do not take it amiss. She has not slept for eight days and eight nights, so great is her desire for you, lord."

Thrym's sister insolently demanded a dowry from the bride. "Give me the red gold rings you're wearing," she said. "Only then will you have my love." But Thrym paid no attention to this. Turning to his servants, he said, "Bring forth Mjollnir, the hammer of Thor. Let my bride put it between her legs"—he laughed obscenely—"and thus will we swear our marriage oath and I will take her to bed."

The servants came back into the hall holding Mjollnir, the hammer of the Thunderer. Thor's heart soared at the sight of his own lost property. Hurling aside the veil he rose and seized the handle of the hammer. He stood revealed before all the astonished hall as Thor the Thunderer, spitter of storms and foe of giants. He swung only once and Thrym fell, his skull smashed to pieces. Then Thor turned to the rest of the company and left not one of them alive in that hall.

The Thrymskvida

The only source for this story is the *Thrymskvida*, one of the poems in the *Poetic Edda*. The story is more humorous than many of the Viking myths, since it turns on Thor's being forced to cross-dress and his deception of Thrym and the rest of the giants. Here Loki plays a generally positive role.

It has been suggested by some scholars that the humor in the story, so uncharacteristic of Viking myth, means that this is more probably a Christian parody of the Scandinavian gods. However, others have suggested that this may, in fact, be among the earliest of the Eddic poems.

THE EYRARLAND STATUE

Among the best-known representations of Thor is one figure known as the Eyrarland statue. It dates from roughly 1000 and shows the god, with a conical helmet, grasping Mjollnir in both hands. It has been suggested by some that this is a depiction of Thor in the moment when he has recovered Mjollnir from Thrym and is preparing to kill the giant and all the rest of the wedding party.

THE THEFT OF IDUNN'S APPLES

Among the most marvelous things found in Asgard were the apples of Idunn. These apples were kept by the goddess Idunn, wife of the god Bragi, and as long as the Æsir and Vanir consumed them, they would never grow old.

The Eagle and the Theft

One day Loki, Odin, and Hoenir were traveling through Midgard. They were hungry and came upon a herd of oxen. Seizing one they butchered it and began to cook it in a cooking pit. After a time, they pulled the meat from the pit, but it was not cooked. Indeed, it might as well never have been in the fire at all.

"This is strange," said Odin the Allfather. They returned the meat to the cooking pit and waited for a time longer. Again they drew it forth, and again it showed no signs of having been cooked. They thrust it back angrily and waited again. Again it remained unchanged.

The three heard a noise from above them and saw an eagle sitting in a tree. "If you are willing to let me eat as much as I will," said the eagle, "I will see to it that your meat is cooked."

The three residents of Asgard discussed this and agreed to the eagle's terms. Then the eagle swept down. "Put the meat back in the pit," it ordered. They did as it demanded, and this time when they took it from the fire, it was cooked to a turn. Appetizing juices ran down its sides, and a fragrant aroma filled the air.

"Now you must fulfill your bargain!" cried the eagle. It opened its beak and gulped down the two thighs and two shoulders of the beast.

"Enough!" roared Loki, springing to his feet. He struck at the bird with his staff. So far he was successful—the bird in surprise and pain dropped the meat and sprang into the air, the staff still sticking in its side. But Loki found he could not let go of the staff and was dragged into the air as well.

He shouted angrily for the bird to release him, but the eagle flapped its wings and flew off, still carrying its burden. It deliberately flew close to the ground so that Loki was smashed into boulders and dragged through the branches of trees as well as thorn bushes that scratched and tore at his body. He shrieked for mercy, but the eagle paid him no heed.

At last the bird spoke to him. "If you wish to be released," it said, "then carry the apples of Idunn out of Asgard." Loki was half weeping with pain, and he swiftly agreed to the eagle's condition.

"In seven days," said the eagle, "lead Idunn across Bifrost at midday." Loki's hands slipped from the staff and he fell to earth. Then he began to walk back toward his companions, planning what he would tell them.

Seven days hence Loki approached Idunn where she was walking, her basket with its magical apples over her arm. "Come with me, Idunn," he said. "I'll show you a marvelous tree I've found."

APPLES IN MYTH

Apples are a popular fruit in mythology. The forbidden fruit in the Garden of Eden is usually depicted as an apple (despite the fact that the Bible nowhere says this was the case). Snow White is poisoned by an apple given to her by her evil stepmother. And Iris, the goddess of discord, used a golden apple to pit the goddesses of the Greeks among one another, leading to the Judgment of Paris and the Trojan War.

Idunn, who was innocent and trusting, accompanied Loki through the gates of Asgard and down the bridge of Bifrost. As soon as they reached Midgard, the sky darkened. Great wings flapped, nearly blowing them over. Claws snatched up Idunn and her apples, and the eagle bore her away to Giant Land. For he was no other than the giant Thiazi in disguise. Idunn screamed and screamed but no one in Asgard could hear her, not even her husband, Bragi.

And now Thiazi gloated over his prize, for he knew that without the magical apples, the gods would grow old and weak, while he could remain young forever.

Without Idunn's apples, the gods grew weaker as old folk do. They began to shrink and to stagger instead of striding over the nine worlds in search of the lost Idunn. Their skins wrinkled and their hands were palsied. Even their minds began to atrophy.

The Council of Odin

Odin pulled himself together as best he might and called a council of the gods. "We must search for Idunn!" he declared. "Without her apples, we are old men and women. Who was the last to see Idunn?"

Heimdall's thrall said, "I saw Loki leading her over Bifrost."

"Loki!" muttered Odin. "The Trickster has done this. We must capture him."

The gods searched for Loki throughout Asgard. At last they discovered him, asleep in Idunn's field, and they bound him and dragged him before Odin. The Allfather sat enthroned in Valaskjálf, his great silver-roofed hall. He glared at Loki. "What have you done with Idunn?" he demanded. "Without her apples, we grow old, you fool! We know you led her out of Asgard. Bring her back, or suffer death!"

"It's true I took her from Asgard," replied Loki. "But I had no choice in the matter." Briefly he told the assembled gods of his encounter with the eagle and of the bargain he had been forced to strike to preserve his own life.

Odin snarled at him in rage. "You didn't have to fulfill that bargain!" he growled. "I should draw a blood eagle on your back and rip your lungs through it."

Loki shrank from the Allfather's anger. "I will find Idunn and her apples and bring her back," he said. "All I ask is that Freyja lend me her falcon shape."

"I will lend you anything you need to bring back the apples," cackled Freyja. Her beautiful face was now wrinkled and cracked with age.

Loki looked at her and laughed. Her hair was falling out. "You are not the most beautiful; now you are bald," he said.

Freyja said nothing but her golden tears trickled down her cheeks. Then Loki crouched and spread his arms wide. Feathers sprang from his back and arms and his nose curved into a sharp beak. As a falcon he sprang into the air and was gone.

The Rescue of Idunn

On and on Loki flew until he reached Thrymheim. Thiazi and his daughter, Skathi, had gone fishing, but Idunn was there, crouched miserably in the hall over the fire. Loki bent his magical powers upon her and changed her into a nut. Then he seized her in his beak and soared out the window.

Moments later Thiazi and his daughter stepped into the room. "Where is Idunn?" roared the giant. "Someone has taken her!" He spied the falcon flying away. "Loki!" he shouted. "Loki has done this thing!" In the blink of an eye he was transformed into his eagle form and he flew after the Trickster.

Faster and faster the two birds flew. Their wings beat against the air so quickly they could scarcely be seen. Odin, seated in his high seat, Hlidskjalf, saw them though, and he cried to the other gods, "Loki is coming!" He ordered the gods to build fires in their halls and to pile shavings against the walls.

Loki soared over the wall surrounding Asgard. Thiazi was just behind him. "Now!" cried Odin. The gods set fire to the shavings. Flames darted up, and Thiazi's wings smoldered and caught fire. With shrieks of agony he fell to the ground, transforming to his own shape. Thor strode up to him and with all his strength brought down his hammer, smashing the giant's skull.

Loki assumed his own shape and dropped the nut at Odin's feet. Smirking at the Allfather, he bent over it and spoke magic. Suddenly Idunn stood before them. She saw the gods and how pitiful they had become. She held out her basket to them, and they took apples from it.

Sources

The story of the theft of Idunn's apples is told in the *Skáldskaparmál* section of the *Prose Edda*, although there are other references to Idunn in the *Poetic Edda*. The basket in which she keeps the apples is made of ash; as we have seen, the ash tree plays an important role in Viking mythology.

The name Idunn is thought to mean "rejuvenator." Both apples and nuts seem to have been important in Norse ritual. For example, baskets of both were found in the Oseberg ship.

THE DEATH OF BALDR

Of all the gods, Baldr was the most beloved and the most beautiful. But he was tormented by dreams that seemed to foretell his death. Odin, his father, determined to find out the meaning of the dream. Mounted on Sleipnir, his swift steed, he traveled from Asgard to the dark, cold depths of Niflheim and to the Gates of Hel itself. There he sought out the mistress of Hel and asked her about the dream.

"Hödr will slay your son," she told him. "Rind will lay with you, and your son by her, Vali, will avenge Baldr. Loki will be bound and he will not break his bonds until Ragnarök. Now go!"

Odin returned to Asgard with a heavy heart and told the results of his visit to his wife, Frigg. She wept many tears over it and then said, "I shall go through the nine worlds and make everything swear an oath never to hurt our son." So she traveled from Asgard to Niflheim. All things swore not to hurt Baldr—water, iron, stone—everything said they would not harm Odin and Frigg's child.

The gods tested the oath. One of them threw a stone at Baldr.

"I don't feel a thing," the god said.

The gods laughed and began throwing other objects at Baldr, but none hurt him. Frigg clapped her hands in delight. Her son was safe.

Now Baldr stood against a wall in Gladsheim, and the gods hurled darts and spears at him. None hurt him. They rebounded and fell at his feet. Even when they struck at him with swords and axes, the metal refused to injure the god.

Loki's Cruelty

Loki alone watched with disdain. His mind turned this way and that, wondering how he could make trouble that was meat and drink to him. At last a plan formed in his mind. He took on the guise of a woman and came to Frigg as she sat in her hall, Fensalir.

"What are the gods doing, O mistress?" he asked.

"They are shooting arrows at Baldr," replied Frigg.

"Why?" asked Loki. "Are you not afraid for your son?"

"Nay," replied the goddess. "For nothing can harm him, for all things have sworn an oath to do him no hurt."

"*All* things, mistress?" asked the woman. Frigg did not hear the eagerness in her voice as she asked this question.

"There is one that I did not ask," Frigg replied. "On my travels I saw a sprout of mistletoe, and I deemed it over-young to swear the oath I required."

Now Loki knew his course of action. He pulled the mistletoe from the earth and carried it to where Hödr stood apart from the gods, who were still playing their game, shooting missiles at Baldr.

"Why do you not take part in this?" Loki asked.

"Because I am blind," replied Hödr.

"No matter," said the scheming Loki. "I will guide your arrow. Shoot with this wand." So saying he gave the mistletoe to Hödr and held the blind god's arms to keep his shot true.

The mistletoe flew from Hödr's bow. It struck Baldr in the chest as the others had done, but to the amazement of the gods, it pierced Baldr's skin. He staggered and fell. Blood gushed from his mouth. His chest rose and fell and was then still.

All the gods cried out in grief at the death of the fairest of them all. They were fain to take vengeance against Hödr for his act, but none wished more violence within the hall.

News was borne to Frigg, and she came, weeping, and bent over the body of her son. "Yet," she said, "perhaps there is still a chance for my poor Baldr. Who among you will ride to Hel and beg the hag to let Baldr return to Asgard?"

There was silence as the gods looked at one another. Then Hermódr, Odin's son, spoke. "I will go," he said. "I will ask for my brother's life back."

The Journey to Hel

Some led forth Odin's eight-legged horse Sleipnir. "Ride this," said Frigg, her face stained with tears, "that you may come to Hel faster. Do not fail me."

"I will not," said Hermódr, and he rode away from Asgard.

Down through the nine worlds he traveled and quickly as he might until he reached the dark, cold reaches of Niflheim. Then he came to the Gates of Hel and banged on them with his fist.

"Who comes to Hel?" said a voice.

"Hermódr of Asgard!"

"What do you seek?"

"I seek an audience with Hel to beg for the soul of my brother, Baldr, fairest of the gods."

The gates swung open, and Hermódr rode into Hel.

The Pyre of Baldr

Meanwhile in Asgard the gods made ready a funeral pyre for Baldr. They brought his body to the sea and placed it in his boat, which was named Hringhorni, greatest of all ships. But when the gods tried to push the boat from the shore, it would not move.

The gods sent word to Giant Land of the difficulty, and soon there came striding across the land the giantess called Hyrrokkin. She grasped the prow of the boat and gave a great push. Fire burst from the rollers beneath it, and the ground trembled, but the boat slid into the water.

Now through the crowd of gods that ringed the shore, Nanna, wife of Baldr burst through. She wept for her lost husband, bending over in agony and letting her tears mingle with the waves. So great was her grief that her heart burst, and she fell down dead. Grieving, the gods lifted her and placed her body on the pyre beside that of her beloved husband.

Now the shore was filled with a great array of gods and others: the Æsir, the Vanir, the frost giants and the hill giants—all these came to watch the burning, so loved was Baldr. Odin stepped onto the ship and from his arm he took the ring called Draupnir and placed it on the pyre.

Thor leaped aboard the boat and thrust a flaming torch into the wood that formed the pyre. He held Mjollnir aloft to hallow the burning. Just then a dwarf ran before him, and in a fury Thor kicked the dwarf so he landed in the fire and was burned up. The smoke from the pyre rose into the sky and spread above the nine worlds, and all mourned the passing of Baldr.

Hermódr's Journey

Now Hermódr was led to the great hall of Hel, and there he beheld Baldr seated among the dead with Nanna beside him. Hermódr lingered there a day and then he came before Hel.

"What do you desire?" she demanded.

"The soul of my brother, Baldr."

"Why?"

"Because of all the gods of Asgard, he is the most loved."

Hel looked at him shrewdly. "Very well," she said. "We will put your words to the test. If all things throughout the nine worlds mourn him and weep for him, he shall return to Asgard. But if some—if one— does not, he shall remain here with me."

Hermódr agreed and began a long journey through the worlds back to Asgard.

When he arrived and told the gods of his journey, Odin sent out messengers through the nine worlds, asking each being, even the earth, wood, and stones, that they pray for Baldr to be released from Hel. So loved was Baldr that all beings and things readily agreed and prayed for Baldr and wept for him.

At last the messengers came to a certain giantess named Thökk in her cave. They begged her to pray and weep for Baldr's return.

She looked at them scornfully and said, "My tears for Baldr will be waterless. Never did I like him, and I will not ask for him to come back. Let Hel hold what she has!"

The messengers, scarcely believing they had heard aright, asked again.

"No!" she cried angrily. "Begone now!"

The messengers returned to Asgard and told Odin and Frigg that alone of all the beings in the nine worlds, Thökk the giantess would not weep for Baldr and so he must remain in Hel.

Odin sat grimly on Hlidskjalf. "Truly," he said, "it seems to me that this giantess has some special reason for hating the gods and Baldr most of all." He pondered and then spoke again. "I believe it was no giantess at all who refused this request. Instead, it was Loki the Trickster, most treacherous of all the folk of Asgard. He shall pay for this."

THE BINDING OF LOKI

The fury of the gods toward Loki knew no bounds. Although he had played tricks on them in the past, none was so cruel as contriving the death of Baldr. Odin was determined to let this happen no more.

Loki heard the rage of the Æsir and Vanir, and he knew he must hide. He fled to a mountain and there he made a house for himself. It had four doors so he could see in all directions. During the day he became a salmon and hid beneath a waterfall, but in the evening he sat before a fire and wove a fishing net.

There was no hiding from Odin as he sat on his high seat of Hlidskjalf. The Æsir raced toward the house, but Loki heard them coming. He cast the net into the fire and, running to the waterfall, became a fish. The Æsir entered the house and searched for him, but he had seemingly vanished.

Then Kvasir, wisest of the gods, noticed that although the net had burned in the fire, it had left a pattern.

"Behold, my brothers!" he said. "The Trickster has become a fish." Then, swiftly, the gods wove their own net after the pattern of that made by Loki. They went to the river and cast it in. Thor held one end and all the Æsir held the other. They drew the net along the river to the waterfall, but crafty Loki had seen it coming and hid between two stones. They drew the net along the river a second time, and this time Loki leaped over the net. Now Thor waded into the water and the gods drew the net toward him. Loki tried to dart past the Thunderer, but Thor seized him and held him by the tail.

THE SALMON'S TAIL

According to the account of this in the *Prose Edda*, this incident is why the salmon's tail tapers toward the end.

Loki's Sons

The gods now set out to capture Loki's sons, Váli and Narfi. When this had been accomplished, Odin changed Váli into the form of a wolf, and Váli tore his brother to pieces. With the guts of Narfi, the gods now bound Loki over three stones. His bonds changed to iron.

The Trickster howled and begged to be released, but the hearts of the gods were adamant. Loki had played them for fools too long. None shed a tear at his fate. They carried him to a dark cave and left him there.

Skathi brought a venomous snake and fastened it above Loki's face so the venom should drip continuously on him. Sigyn, Loki's wife, entered the cave and stared at her husband, bound and helpless. Then she produced a wooden bowl with which to catch the venom. When at last the bowl was full, she carried it away to pour into a rocky basin, and the venom dripped over Loki's face until she returned.

And so Loki was bound, and so he will remain bound until the coming of Ragnarök.

Chapter Eleven

SIGURD THE VOLSUNG

Sigurd is the central hero of the *Völsunga Saga*. Although the version of the saga that we have today was composed in the thirteenth century, it clearly reflects much older traditions, ones that would have been known to the Vikings. Many of the poems in the *Poetic Edda* are concerned with characters in the story.

The tale contains many of the elements of traditional Viking mythology: angry gods, a young man with a divine destiny, mysterious artifacts, and a magical sword. It also tells a sad love story—sad because the love of Brynhild for Sigurd goes unfulfilled—and speaks of a cursed treasure.

In the late nineteenth century, the story was the subject of a long poem by the great pre-Raphaelite painter, writer, and craftsman William Morris, who published it as *The Story of Sigurd the Volsung and the Fall of the Niblungs.* The story played a considerable role in shaping the fiction of Tolkien, as can be seen in many common elements: the sword that is passed from father to son, the young man seeking to avenge the death of his ancestors, and so on.

THE VOLSUNGS

Sigurd's story is only part of the larger tale told in the saga, one describing the rise and fall of the Volsungs. The story begins with an account of Sigi, a son of Odin. Sigi had killed a thrall, Bregi, because he was jealous of him, and for this he was forced out of his lands. But he dwelt apart and still became mighty. He had a son, Rerir, who in turn bore a son, Volsung, who became king over Hunland and a mighty man in his own right.

Volsung wedded a giant's daughter, Ljod, and they had ten sons and one daughter. Of the son, one was named Sigmund, and the daughter Signy. They were accounted the fairest in all the land as well as the wisest. And Volsung built a great hall; within it was a tree whose branches stemmed out and merged with the roof beams, and the tree was called Branstock.

The king of Gothland, Siggeir, begged for the hand of Signy in marriage. Volsung was reluctant at first, but his daughter pleaded with him as well, and at last he acceded.

On the day of the wedding, as the wedding guests gathered in Sigmund's hall, a man entered whom none recognized. He bore a great sword, and without a word to anyone he walked up to Branstock and smote it a blow. The sword sank into the roof tree to the hilt. Then the man said, "Whoso draweth this sword from this stock, shall have the same as a gift from me, and shall find in good sooth that never bare he better sword in hand than is this." At this the old man departed, and none knew from where he came.

All the men in the hall set their hands to the sword, but none could draw it forth from the roof tree. Then Sigmund, son of Volsung, laid hands on it. His muscles strained, and sweat burst forth on his brow, and with a mighty heave he pulled the sword from the tree. Some of those present offered to buy the sword from him, but he refused, declaring that since he had drawn it forth, it was his to keep and his alone to wield.

THE SWORD IN THE STONE

Students of Arthurian legend will recognize the parallels to the story of Excalibur, Arthur's sword, which was set in a stone with the injunction that only the true king of England could pull it from the rock. Eventually, although many tried, Arthur succeeded and was thereby acclaimed ruler of England.

The Treachery of Siggeir

Signy recognized almost immediately that she had made a mistake in wedding Siggeir, for she detected a rottenness in his heart. She begged her father to annul the marriage, but Volsung refused, and Siggeir and Signy returned to Gothland. Siggeir asked Volsung and his sons to visit the couple in three months. So at the appointed time, Volsung and his sons sailed to Gothland and were welcomed by Siggeir.

But Signy drew her father aside and told him that Siggeir planned to strike them when they were unprepared. "Wherefore," she said, "you must return over the sea and only come back when you have assembled the greatest army that may be."

Sternly, her father reminded her that he had sworn an oath never to flee any foe. Signy began to weep and begged that she might not go back to her husband, but her father declared, "You shall return to him as his wife, no matter how matters fare with us."

The next day, as Signy had warned, Siggeir fell upon them and would have slain them all had they not been ready for his coming. Eight times, Volsung and his sons stormed through Siggeir's line, slaying and destroying. But at last Volsung fell among his folk and his ten sons were captured by the enemy.

Now Signy prayed to her lord and husband that her brothers might not be slain outright but that they should be placed in stocks. Grudgingly Siggeir agreed, and a great beam was laid across the legs of the brothers, who sat under it in a deep place of the woods.

At midnight, there came from the woods an old she-wolf of evil aspect, and she seized one of the brothers in her teeth and tore his body asunder. She devoured all of it before slinking off into the forest.

The next day, Signy learned of what had happened. Yet she was powerless to prevent a recurrence of the tragedy. For each night, the she-wolf reappeared, and each dawn another brother was dead. Now, when only Sigmund remained, Signy had an idea about how to save her remaining brother. She sent a messenger to Sigmund with a jar of honey. Sigmund spread the honey all over his face and put some in his mouth.

When the she-wolf came that night, she smelled the honey. She began to lick Sigmund's face. He kept his body rigid as the wolf's foul tongue licked him, devouring the honey. Then the she-wolf reached her tongue into Sigmund's mouth to taste the honey therein. Quick as a flash, Sigmund clamped his teeth around the wolf's tongue. The wolf struggled to free herself, but Sigmund held on tighter, and at last the wolf's tongue was wrenched from her jaws. Howling, she fled into the forest, and Sigmund spat the tongue onto the ground. Some say the wolf was the mother of Siggeir and that she had been turned into a wolf by the enchantment of a troll.

Sigmund's Son

Sigmund, freed from the threat of the she-wolf, contrived to loose himself from the stocks. When Signy heard what had happened, she came to him, where he was living in the forest. Then she carried to the king the falsehood that all the Volsungs were dead.

Siggeir and Signy had two sons. When the eldest was ten years old, his mother sent him to Sigmund. But Sigmund tested him for his will and his nerve, and the lad failed the test. Sigmund sent word of this to his sister. "Kill him then," said Signy. "For why should such a one live longer." And her brother did so. Later Signy sent the other son to Sigmund, and the same thing befell.

A witch woman came to the court of Siggeir, and Signy took her aside and asked her to change places and to change their appearances so that the king might be deceived. This the witch did, and while the witch woman stayed in the bed of the king, Signy in the guise of the witch went to the house of her brother. She told him she was a wandering woman and asked for shelter.

Sigmund agreed, and that night he and the witch woman lay in one another's arms in the forest. Then Signy returned to the court and rejoined her husband's side in her own guise.

Nine months later, Signy brought forth a son named Sinfjotli. This son too, when he was of age, she sent to Sigmund. But this time the boy passed Sigmund's tests, and Sigmund knew him for a true Volsung.

Sigmund's Revenge

Sinfjotli remained with Sigmund until he was an adult. Then the two decided it was time to avenge Sigmund's father. They came to the king's palace, but they were sighted by the king and Signy's two young sons, who were playing with a ball, and the boys told their father there were two strange men in the palace.

Signy bade her brother slay the children but he refused. Then Sinfjotli drew his dagger and killed them both. Siggeir called for his men and the two heroes were overwhelmed.

Siggeir, thinking of what was the worst fate he could bestow on them, decided they would be entombed. A great rock tomb was built, but it was divided in half by a stone, and Sigmund was placed on one side of the stone and Sinfjotli on the other. But before the lid was placed on the tomb to seal in the men, Signy threw down some straw to Sinfjotli. Concealed in it was Sigmund's sword. He thrust it through the rock, and Sigmund caught the point, and between the two they sawed through the barrier.

They freed themselves easily from the tomb, using the sword, and went to Siggeir's hall wherein he and all his men were sleeping. They kindled a great fire, and the king and his followers woke to billowing clouds of smoke.

"Who has done this?" cried the king.

"I, Sigmund, son of Volsung," roared Sigmund, "and know that not all the Volsungs are dead." Then he called, "Come out here, sister, and stand by your kin."

Signy did as he bade. She looked at Siggeir and said to him, "In vengeance for my father, whom I loved, I ordered the slaying of your sons of my body. And here is Sinfjotli, who is not thy son but mine and my brother's, son of two Volsungs. Now I am avenged, for none I brought forth of my accursed marriage lives. Now I can die." So saying, she went back into the smoke and flames and died with her husband and his men.

SUTTEE

Although Signy's decision to die in the fire with her treacherous husband may strike us as odd, it would have seemed perfectly sensible to the Vikings who heard the story. The practice of suttee—the burning of a dead man's wife on his funeral pyre—was, according to H.R. Ellis Davidson, "practiced in Sweden in honor of Odin until the tenth century."

HELGI

Sigmund and Sinfjotli returned to the land of the Volsungs, and Sigmund took up the throne. He had two sons, Helgi and Hamund. When Helgi was born, the Norns came to his bedside and told his father that his son would be the mightiest of all kings. When Helgi was only fifteen, he became a leader of the army, and Sinfjotli was his supporter.

Helgi was a successful warrior, and he won the love of a woman named Sigrun. He fought many battles in which he was victorious. But Sinfjotli fell, poisoned through the treachery of a woman.

Sigmund at last fell wounded in battle, his sword broken beneath him. Then his wife, Hjordis, came to him and asked him if he might be healed. He replied that "Odin does not will that I draw sword again." But, he said, "You are great with a man-child. Nourish him well, for he will be the mightiest of our race and keep for him the shards of my sword that it may be forged anew for his hand. When he died, a band of Vikings led by the Alf, son of King Hjalprek of Denmark, happened by the field of battle. They took Sigmund's treasure, and they also took Hjordis, and when they came back to Denmark, she became Alf's wife and had much honor in the land.

THE YOUNG SIGURD

In the due course of time Hjordis delivered her child, and he was named Sigurd. The boy was raised in the household of the king, and all who met him remarked on his strength and beauty. Sigurd was taught all manner of arts, how to play chess, how to speak in many languages, and the secret of runes.

When Sigurd came of age, he desired a horse. He came to the king and asked for one. "Choose one to your liking," said the king. Sigurd went out to where the horses were grazing, and there he met an old man, clad in gray. "What are you doing, Sigurd," asked the man.

"Choosing a horse," replied the youth.

"Come with me then," said the man. They went to the river called Busil-tarn, and there on the bank Sigurd beheld a steed gray and young and of great power and beauty. "I choose that one!" he cried.

"You have chosen well," said the old man. "He is kin to Sleipnir, Odin's horse, and his name is Grani. There is none like him. May he bear you to fortune." Though Sigurd did not know it, the old man was Odin himself.

Regin and Andvari's Hoard

While he was a boy, Sigurd had been raised by a cunning old man named Regin. One day Regin said to him, "It's a pity you do not have more wealth. I know of a great hoard for the winning, and there is much honor and fame you would win, along with gold."

Sigurd bade him explain himself, so Regin told him.

Regin was the third of three sons of a man named Hreidmar; the first son was named Fafnir and the second Otter. Regin was skilled in the working of iron and gold, while Otter was a great fisherman who had the form of an otter during the day. But Fafnir was grim and desired all things be his.

There was a dwarf named Andvari, who lived beneath a waterfall, disguised as a pike, and in this guise he ate as many fish as he pleased. He possessed a great hoard of gold that he kept secret. Otter, it happened, was accustomed to hunt fish around that waterfall as well and lay them on the bank. One day, he caught a great salmon and left it on the bank. He devoured it, but as he did so, Loki and Odin happened along. Loki, seeing an otter eating a salmon, cast a stone at the creature and killed it. The gods flayed the otter's skin and bore it with them. That night they came to Hreidmar's house and told him what they had done. "Alas!" he cried. "You have slain my son, whom I loved."

He told them they must pay a ransom, and for that ransom they must fill the otter skin with gold and cover it in red gold and bring it to him.

RED GOLD

Red gold is an alloy of pure gold. It is made up of 75 percent gold and 25 percent copper. It was very popular for a time in Russia, for which reason it is sometimes called Russian gold.

The gods knew they needed gold, and Odin knew of the hoard of Andvari. So he sent Loki to get the gold. Loki came to the waterfall and cast a net into the waters. The pike swam into the net, and Loki taunted the pike, saying,

> What fish of all fishes
> Swims strong in the flood
> But hath learned little wit to beware?
> Thine head must thou buy
> From abiding in Hel
> And find me the wan waters' flame.

Andvari changed from his pike shape to that of a dwarf. Grumbling and cursing his ill luck, he led the Trickster to his hoard. Loki took the hoard down to the last ring. Enraged, the dwarf cried out that the gold from now until forever was cursed; ill fortune would come to all who owned it. They brought the gold in the otter skin back to Hreidmar as wergild for his slain son. Loki warned Hreidmar:

> Gold enow, gold enow,
> A great wergild, thou hast
> That my head in good hap I may hold;
> But thou and thy sons
> Are naught fated to thrive,
> The bane shall it be of you both.

Loki's words were shortly fulfilled, for Fafnir, greed growing in his heart, slew his father and seized the gold. Lying with it, trusting no man, he became a dragon and now lies still guarding the hoard that Loki stole from the dwarf.

Sigurd's Sword

Sigurd listened intently to Regin's words, and a flame awoke in his heart to go forth and slay the dragon, foul wyrm that it was, and restore to Regin what was rightfully his. But to undertake such a quest, he needed a sword. Regin attempted to forge one for him, but he failed in the attempt. Then Sigurd brought forth the shards of the sword of Sigmund, and these pieces Regin forged together. The sword was called Gram after the wishes of Sigmund.

Now Regin wished Sigurd to slay the wyrm Fafnir, but Sigurd first wished to avenge his father Sigmund. So he gathered an army and traveled to the land of the sons of King Hunding, against whom Sigmund had fallen in battle. There were mighty conflicts, but Sigurd had the mastery, for none could stand before Gram. One of the sons, Lyngi the king, led a great army as well, but Sigurd met him in battle and clave him right through, from the crown of his head through his body. So the Volsungs were avenged upon their enemies.

The Death of Fafnir

Now Sigurd was ready to pit himself against the dragon Fafnir. He and Regin rode to the place where the dragon guarded his hoard. Sigurd knew the blood of dragons was deadly, and he said to Regin, "This wyrm appears to be of great size. How shall I overcome him?"

"Dig a hole," answered his mentor. "Climb into the hole and when he comes to water, stab at him from beneath."

"But what about his blood?" protested Sigurd. "It may destroy me even as I am in the hole."

"If you are afraid of everything," sneered Regin, "perhaps you had better run home."

Sigurd said nothing more until they reached the place. Then Regin turned and rode away, for he was very afraid.

An old man appeared to Sigurd, who told him of the advice of his tutor. "Nay, nay!" said the old man. "Dig many holes that will hold the blood of the wyrm and crawl into one of them. Let the wyrm's blood flow into the other pits when you stab it in the heart. Thus will you slay the beast."

Now Fafnir crawled down to his watering place. Sigurd, with Gram in his hand, thrust upward and caught the dragon under its left shoulder. The creature shrieked and thrashed at the stroke, and its blood spilled and ran into the pits Sigurd had dug.

CLASSIC ILLUSTRATION

The great nineteenth–early twentieth-century illustrator Arthur Rackham drew a picture of Sigurd's fight with Fafnir. The illustration was part of the book *Siegfried and the Twilight of the Gods* (Siegfried is a German variant of Sigurd).

Fafnir knew he had his death wound, and he spoke then to Sigurd, asking him who he was and how he came there. Sigurd replied warily, and then Fafnir said to him, "Little good will that gold that you seek do you, for it brings a curse on all who possess it."

"Nonetheless," said Sigurd, "I ride now to your lair to take your hoard that you have so jealously guarded these years."

"Ride, then," said the dying dragon, "and you will find gold enough to last you all the rest of your days. Yet that gold shall be your bane and the bane of everyone who finds and takes it." And with that, he shuddered in his death agonies and expired.

The Death of Regin

Now Regin came up to Sigurd and praised his deed. But Sigurd said contemptuously, "You observed my battle from the safety of a hedgerow. You took no part in it."

"If the sword I forged for you was not good enough service," retorted Regin, "I do not know what other help I might have rendered. But now the wyrm is dead, please, I beg you, cut out its heart and roast it so I may eat it."

Sigurd cut out the dragon's heart and began to cook it. The blood sizzled in the pan and some of it spat out on Sigurd's fingers. He licked them, and at once he could understand the speech of the birds. And the woodpeckers chattered at him, "You are roasting that heart for another, Sigurd, but you should eat it yourself." Another said, "Regin tried to entrap you. He contrived at your death, while using you to slay his brother." And another said, "Wiser would it be to slay Regin, take the hoard, and ride over Hindfell where sleeps Brynhild."

Hearing them, and realizing the truth of their words, Sigurd drew Gram and with a single stroke he swept off the head of Regin. Then he ate some of the dragon's heart and leaping on his horse he rode along the wyrm's trail until he reached its lair. There he found a vast pile of gold and jewels. He loaded it in two great boxes and set them on his horse. Then, heeding the advice of the birds, he rode toward Hindfell.

Chapter Twelve

SIGURD AND BRYNHILD

The tale of Sigurd and his destruction of the dragon Fafnir would be impressive for any hero. But Sigurd also forms half of one of the great tragic love stories in northern mythology—the tale of Brynhild.

After defeating Fafnir and ransacking his golden hoard, and after slaying the treacherous Regin, Sigurd rode a long way south until he came to the lands of the Franks. There he came to the gates of a great castle, all hung about with shields and with a brave banner flying from the topmost turret.

SIGURD'S DISCOVERY OF BRYNHILD

Sigurd entered the castle and was challenged by no guard, for the place seemed deserted. Yet at last he came upon a knight, clad in full armor, lying upon a bier. The knight seemed to be sleeping, and no efforts of Sigurd could rouse him.

Then Sigurd took off the sleeping knight's helm. And behold! It was no man but a woman of great beauty. Now Sigurd took his sword, Gram, with which he had slain Fafnir, and he cut through the armor as easily as if it had been cloth.

Then she awoke and asked him, "Are you then Sigurd Sigmundson, carrying Fafnir's helm in his hand? And is that sword in your hand Fafnir's bane?"

He replied, "Sigmund's son has done the deed. Of the Volsung am I. But I have heard that you are daughter of a mighty king, and folk say you are lovely and full of lore."

Then Brynhild told Sigurd how she came to be asleep there. She said, "Two kings fought, one of them named Helm Gunnar. To him had Odin promised victory. His foe was Agnar. I smote down Helm Gunnar, for I was a shieldmaiden. Then Odin was angered that I had made false his promise. He struck me with a sleeping thorn. Never again, he said, should I have the victory but instead should be given in marriage. Thereupon I swore that I would never wed until I met one who did not know fear."

BRYNHILD AND EOWYN

Tolkien drew on Brynhild in shaping the character of Éowyn in *The Lord of the Rings*. Like Brynhild, Éowyn wishes to be a shieldmaiden and not to be reduced to the lot of women in a male-dominated society. As Brynhild longs for Sigurd, so Éowyn wishes for the love of Aragorn. Toward the end of the novel, however, she recognizes that love is for Aragorn's position rather than for himself, and she marries Faramir, warden of Ithilien. Again, there are significant parallels to the way in which the story of Sigurd and Brynhild develops.

Sigurd asked Brynhild to teach him her lore. She brought him a cup of ale and said, "I will teach you runes of war; cut them on the hilt of your sword. I will teach you runes of seafaring; cut them on the rudder of your ship. I will teach you word runes; weave them into cloth and cast it about you. And I will teach you ale runes; carve them into your drinking horn."

Sigurd replied:

> Ne'er shall I flee,
> Though thou wottest [thinkest] me fey;
> Never was I born for blenching,
> Thy loved rede [advice] will I
> Hold aright in my heart
> Even as long as I may live.

Brynhild's Advice

Brynhild began to teach Sigurd wisdom. "Be kind to friends and kin," she said, "and do not reward their trespasses against you. Do not allow your mind to dwell overlong on foolish words spoken by men at gatherings of the folk. If you fare by places thronged with evil, take care, and let not fair women beguile you while you are feasting. Never swear a false oath, for harsh is the penalty for oath-breaking. Do not trust one whose father, son, or kin you have slain, for even among the young a wolf may take shape."

Sigurd was amazed at her wisdom and said to her, "Never among the sons of men is there one as wise as you. I would have you for my beloved."

Brynhild replied, "I would choose you as well, though I had all men's sons to choose from." And so they plighted their troth to one another.

Brynhild's Prophecy

Sigurd rode to Hlymdale where dwelt the mighty chief Heimir, father of Brynhild and her sister Bekkhild. There Sigurd was welcomed and he stayed, hunting and feasting with those of the household. At length, Brynhild came there as well, and she sat with other maidens and told them of the deeds of Sigurd and the slaying of the wyrm Fafnir. And the women wove great tapestries depicting these brave deeds. Sigurd came upon her sitting in a bower and cast his arms around her. "Now it has come to pass," he said, "even as you promised." Then he drank from a horn she gave him and kissed her and said, "You are the fairest that was ever born."

But Brynhild looked sorrowfully at him. "Wiser it would be," she said, "not to cast love and troth into a woman's power, for ever they shall break that which they have promised."

"What do you mean?" he asked.

She answered, "It is not allowed by the fates that we should be together. I am a shieldmaiden and must wear a helm and fight in battle. Nor is the prospect displeasing to me."

Sigurd said, "What offspring of our love can there be if we do not live together?"

She shook her head and said, "I shall look upon the hosts of kings, but you shall wed Gudrun, daughter of Giuki."

Sigurd laughed and said, "You are mistaken. What king's daughter lives to beguile me? I am not double-hearted, and I swear to you that I shall have you for my own and none other." Then he gave her a golden ring, and he swore again his love for her.

RINGS IN NORSE MYTHOLOGY

Rings were extremely important to the Vikings, both as magical objects and as wealth in their own right. Large numbers of rings have been found in Viking hoards. Some few of them carried runic carvings, evidently of mystical import. Odin wore an arm ring, Draupnir. Another ring, the Andvaranaut, was the Ring of Nibelung.

Gudrun, Giuki's Daughter

Sigurd rode to the hall of Giuki, who was a chief whose dwelling was south of the Rhine River. There Giuki welcomed him, and Sigurd noticed the beauty of Giuki's daughter Gudrun.

Giuki's wife Grimhild listened closely to Sigurd's tale of his adventures, and she marked how he spoke of Brynhild and his love for her. She marked also the chests of gold he carried with him. And she thought it would be well if he forgot Brynhild and instead wed her daughter Gudrun. So she brewed an enchanted ale and brought it to him in a great horn, saying to him, "Great joy do you bring us by abiding here. Now drink from this horn."

Sigurd drank a great draught, and as he did so, memory of Brynhild departed from him. And each night he drank, and each night Gudrun seemed more lovely to him. After five seasons dwelling in that place, he was well content, and Giuki said, "All things will we do for you as long as you abide here. And you shall have my daughter unasked for, though many men have demanded her hand and left disappointed."

Sigurd thanked him heartily, and the two men swore brotherhood to one another. Sigurd and Gudrun were wedded, and so Brynhild's prophecy was fulfilled. Sigurd gave his bride some of the dragon heart to eat, and so she became wise. They had a son whom they named Sigmund in memory of Sigurd's father.

The Wooing of Brynhild

Now Grimhild went to her son Gunnar and advised him to woo Brynhild. Gunnar agreed and he and his followers rode to Hlymdale along with Sigurd. There Heimir gave them a good welcome. Gunnar told him of his errand, and Heimir said, "Brynhild shall not wed any that she herself has not chosen. But I will tell you this: Her hall is but a little way from here, and it is in the midst of a castle roofed with shields. But around the hall is a ring of fire. If you can pass through that fire and come to her, I believe she will have you."

Gunnar and the others who had come with him traveled to Brynhild's hall, and Gunnar spurred his horse, but the animal would not move.

"Why aren't you going to her, Gunnar?" Sigurd asked.

"My horse will not approach the flames," replied Gunnar. "Lend me your horse, Grani."

"Certainly," replied Sigurd. But even now, Grani would not move toward the fire.

Then Sigurd and Gunnar performed a magic and each assumed the likeness of the other. And disguised as Gunnar, Sigurd mounted Grani and rode toward the fire.

At first the fire rose with a great roar, deafening those who watched. But then it sank down and Sigurd passed through it without hurt.

Brynhild asked, "What man is it?"

"Gunnar, son of Giuki," Sigurd replied. "You are awarded me as wife by the will and goodwill of your father, for I have ridden through the flames as you said the man must do who would win your hand."

"I do not know what to answer," she said.

"Answer yes, for this you have sworn to do."

She agreed and led him to her chamber, where he remained for three nights. But he laid the sword Gram between them, and when she asked why he said he had sworn to do so.

She took off her ring, Andvaranaut, and gave it to him, and he gave her another ring from Fafnir's hoard. Then he went back to his followers, and he and Gunnar restored their original shapes.

Brynhild went back to the hall of her father and there she confessed to her father than she saw past the deception and knew it was Sigurd, not Gunnar, who had come to her. But Heimir said things must proceed as fated. So Brynhild and Gunnar were married, and a great feast was held to celebrate the wedding.

FEATURES OF THE VÖLSUNGA SAGA

The story of Sigurd, his ancestry, his killing of the dragon Fafnir, and his love for and abandonment of Brynhild form the first part of the *Völsunga*. This is an Icelandic saga, but like practically all the literature of early Iceland it reflects much older traditions. Although Sigurd is the central character in the story, it is clear that as a whole, the saga reflects the fortunes of the Volsungs, a large and—one presumes—at one time important clan. The story illustrates many of the features of

Viking literature: the capriciousness of fate (sadly, Brynhild knows from the beginning that her love for Sigurd and his for her is destined to be unfulfilled); the primacy of family honor (Signy is willing to destroy her own offspring to claim vengeance upon the man who slaughtered her father and her brothers); the unreliability of surface appearances (the shape-shifting Sigurd and Gunnar, as well as the strong possibility that the she-wolf who kills the imprisoned brothers is the mother of Siggeir). In addition there is the violence, an essential part of storytelling in a violent, brutal society. The dragon guarding its hoard bears some resemblance to the dragon slain by the Geatish hero Beowulf in his last deed as king (see Chapter 13).

Although the tale ends on a high note—the wedding of Brynhild and Gunnar—the *Völsunga* ends tragically. When Brynhild and Gudrun quarrel over who has the better husband, Gudrun tells Brynhild the truth of what happened and the deception that was played upon her. Brynhild has already guessed part of it, but now she confronts Sigurd and charges him with using her. In a rage, she kills his son by Gudrun, Sigmund. Gunnar and his brother plot to kill Sigurd, and they enchant their younger brother Guttorm to do the deed. Guttorm attacks Sigurd while the latter is in bed, and both men are killed, a sad end for the epic hero. It is revealed that the source of all this strife is the ring Andvaranaut, which, unbeknownst to Sigurd, was accursed and would cause dissension among any who possessed it. Finally Brynhild orders a funeral pyre be built for Sigurd, Guttorm, and Sigmund. As the flames are rising, she casts herself on the fire. She and Sigurd are united in death as they were not in life.

Elements of the story worked their way down through German literature. Sigurd became transformed to Siegfried, the hero of the epic *Nibelung*. This story retained elements of the Viking myth: Siegfried was the slayer of a dragon, but bathing in its blood had made him immortal.

He wishes to marry the Kriemhild, sister of King Gunther of the Burgundians, and in return helps Gunther woo Brünhild by employing the same strategy used in the *Völsunga*'s account.

From there, matters fall out much as they did in the *Völsunga*: Brünhild and Kriemhild quarrel, the argument spills over to their husbands, and Siegfried is slain treacherously (he is speared in the back, the one place that the dragon's blood did not cover and thus the only spot through which he is vulnerable). His gold is thrown into the Rhine River to prevent him from raising an army with it.

Wagner and The Ring of the Nibelung

Between 1848 and 1874, the composer Richard Wagner (1813–1883) composed a cycle of four operas telling the story of Siegfried and Brünhild. Elements of the Viking myth have now been shifted further, although Germanized versions of the Norse gods appear as characters in the operas. The key to the tragedy lies in the Ring of Nibelung, forged by the dwarf Alberich from gold stolen from the Rhine maidens. The ring is cursed, just as is Andvaranaut, and brings ill luck and strife to any who hold it. Odin (called here Wotan) steals the ring from the dwarf with help from Loki (Loge) but must give it to the giants Fafner and Fasolt, who built Valhalla for the gods. Siegfried has become Odin's grandson and is tasked with recovering the ring for the gods. This he does by slaying Fafner but is eventually killed through treachery. Finally, Brünhild is a Valkyrie and Odin's daughter (which would seem to preclude her becoming the lover of his grandson, but never mind).

The four operas are:

1. *The Rhinegold*
2. *The Valkyrie*
3. *Siegfried*
4. *The Twilight of the Gods*

WAGNER AND THE NAZIS

Wagner's operas were seen by the Germans in the late nineteenth and early twentieth centuries as an expression of "Germanness," especially since the Germans had only been united as a nation in the last quarter of the nineteenth century. Added to the fact that Wagner was a confirmed anti-Semite, it was perhaps inevitable that his work should have become a favorite of Adolf Hitler. There is considerable irony, therefore, that as Russian armies crashed into Berlin in the spring of 1945 and the Thousand Year Reich of the Nazis was collapsing around them, the Berlin Philharmonic chose to stage a performance of the musical score from *Götterdämmerüng—The Twilight of the Gods*.

Chapter Thirteen

BEOWULF

This tale of the north is among the most well known of Scandinavian myths. One can imagine a crowd of men sitting around a fire, faces shining in the yellow light, listening as a skald recites this tale of heroism and death.

Hrothgar, king of the Danes, was moved to build a great hall to show his power and wealth. So he erected the hall and named it Heorot.

> A gabled mead hall   fashioned by craftsmen
> Which the sons of men   should hear of forever,
> And there within   he would share out
> Among young and old   all God had given him,
> Except common land   and the lives of men.

So the hall was built and warriors gathered in it to celebrate with mugs of mead and to tell stories of war and victory and death. But that night, when all slept, a monster came creeping out of the marshes that surrounded Heorot. His name was Grendel, and he was outside the race of men, cast away and bitter. Into the great hall he crept and seized thirty of the slumbering nobles and fled back with them to his lair, where he slaughtered them and devoured their bodies.

So began Grendel's attacks on Heorot, and Hrothgar and his followers were helpless to stop them. For twelve years they continued. And Hrothgar brooded on how to prevent the attacks and restore peace to his hall.

Across the sea, word of the attacks reached the ears of Beowulf, a thane of the Geats. He chose from among his followers the bravest and best, and in their longship they set off for Heorot.

THE BATTLE WITH GRENDEL

A watchman on the shore, a retainer of Hrothgar, saw them land and greeted them. "Never have I seen such mighty men!" he said admiringly. "But assure me you're not spies."

Beowulf told him from whence they came. "We are come to the aid of Hrothgar," he said. "For I have a plan to defeat the monster and restore Hrothgar to his seat in Heorot."

Word was sent to Hrothgar, who said, "I knew this man when he was a boy. Ecgtheow was his sire. I would like to see what kind of man he has become." And he bade Beowulf come in to his presence.

Beowulf made his obeisance to the king and said, "Dear lord, I have come to rid you of this scourge. I ask only that you allow me and my followers to contest with Grendel. The monster, it is said, carries no weapons, and neither shall I. I shall best him strength for strength or perish trying."

Hrothgar had no choice but to agree. He ordered food and drink brought for his guests and joined them in feasting and merry-making. Then at last he and his people retired to their beds, and Beowulf and his men sat in the hall awaiting Grendel.

It was a long vigil, and one by one the men dropped off to sleep. At last, when all was silent, a shadow entered the hall: Grendel. He crept toward one of the sleeping men and reached out a hand to seize him. But Beowulf, who had only been pretending to sleep, sprang up and with a grip of iron clamped his hand around the monster's.

Around and around the hall they wrestled. Beowulf's men, wakened now, shouted encouragement and clashed sword upon shield, but none dared join the affray. Sometimes Beowulf had the upper hand, and sometimes Grendel almost bore him to the earth.

Grendel grew tired. This was like no foe he had ever faced before, and daylight was coming. He gave a great cry of despair and pain and Beowulf, with an effort, wrenched his arm and tore it from his shoulder. Then Grendel fled back shrieking to his lair to linger in pain and die.

Beowulf's men crowded round, cheering their leader. The warrior himself found a rope and tied it around Grendel's arm. He threw the end over one of the beams in the hall and as Hrothgar and his followers entered Heorot they found Beowulf pulling up Grendel's arm to the ceiling as the rays of the morning sun shone down on him and turned his figure all to gold.

GRENDEL'S MOTHER

After celebrating the defeat of Grendel with many horns of sweet-tasting mead, Hrothgar, his men, and the visiting Geats settled down to what they hoped would be an unbroken night of sleep. But it was not to be. In the dark of the night, Grendel's mother, mourning the loss of her son and herself a frightful monster, broke in upon them. She carried off Æschere, of all the Geats the most beloved of Beowulf.

Hrothgar told the grieving warrior that Grendel's mother made her dwelling at the bottom of a deep pool.

> Not a pleasant place!
> Tearing waves   start up from that spot,
> Black against the sky,   while the gloomy wind
> Stirs awful storms   till the air turned choking,
> The heavens weep.

Together, Beowulf and his companions made their way to the mere wherein Grendel and his mother dwelt. A harsh place it was, ringed with swamps and foul-smelling air and stirred ever and again by winds. Then Unferth, who had dared to doubt Beowulf's courage when they drank at Heorot together regretted of his hasty words. He offered Beowulf his sword, Hrunting, to combat the monster's mother. So holding the sword, Beowulf sank beneath the waters, and his men sat and waited on the banks above.

Down, down Beowulf plunged, through the murky waters. At last he came to a deep grotto, many feet below the surface where his men waited anxiously. There, at last, he drew breath and plunged into the rocky cave, seeking his foe.

Foul was the air he breathed, and as he strode along the rocky corridors, dark and far from the world of men, he encountered the ghastly remains of the heroes slain by Grendel in his forays above ground. Here was an arm; there was a leg. All were bloody and torn.

Now at last he encountered more and more remains until the way opened before him and he found himself in a great cavern. There at last lay Grendel's body, his arm wrenched from him by Beowulf's might. The monster's body was surrounded by more bodies, those whom he and his mother had slain. But Beowulf, unafraid, leaped into the cave, and from the shadows, Grendel's mother sprang, seeking to avenge her son's death.

Beowulf hewed great strokes upon her with Hrunting, but in vain for the sword could not pierce her flesh. Around and around the cave the two circled, striking ever and anon at one another. In fury Beowulf cast the useless sword from him and grappled with her, but she was stronger than her son and bested him. Then Beowulf gave a great cry and, seeing a sword resting by her, snatched it up and struck at her. Through her neck the sword sang, and she fell, lying by the side of her ill-begotten son. Beowulf, slayer of monsters, hero of the Geats, lifted the sword and struck off Grendel's head as proof of his great deeds. Yet even as he did so, the sword he held failed in his hand and the blade sizzled and burned like a brand. In smoke it dissolved, so foul was the monster's blood from which it drank.

Holding the hilt in one hand and Grendel's head in the other, Beowulf plunged once more into the foul water of the mere. Up and up he swam until he saw above him the light of a brightening day. Then his head burst the surface and his despairing men gave a great shout of joy when they saw he was returned to them victorious.

THE BATTLE WITH THE DRAGON

Beowulf and the Geats returned to their own lands with the good will of Hrothgar and his people. For many years, Beowulf lived there until he rose to be king of the Geats.

After many years—half a century at least—a slave stole a cup from the massed hoard of a dragon who dwelt on the borders of the land. The dragon's rage knew no bounds, and he laid waste to all the land around his lair. Beowulf and his trusty warriors left their mead hall and declared they would challenge the dragon. But Beowulf, last and best of heroes, declared to his companions that he alone would face the beast. He challenged the dragon, and the beast struck at him with claw and fire. Round and round he and the dragon struggled, and all his companions, fearing for their lives, fled. One alone stayed with him, Wiglaf the faithful, shield bearer. He remained with his liege lord, supporting him and at last he and Beowulf, mighty in war, slew the dragon and struck off its head to be a token of the valiant.

CUPS AND THIEVES

It's really impossible to read much in the way of Scandinavian mythology and not keep coming back to J.R.R. Tolkien. In this case, of course, there's the story of the thief who steals a cup from a dragon hoard; anyone who's read *The Hobbit* is already sitting up and saying, "Hello!"

But Beowulf was wounded unto the death and, as Wiglaf chanted in despair a song to the gods, Beowulf the mighty gave up his spirit and went to join his fathers in the halls of Valhalla.

Then the returning warriors, shamed by their actions, built a great pyre and placed upon it the body of their king, Beowulf, and burned him so that he might join his forefathers. From the sea there was still visible a barrow in which the remains of the king, mightiest of the Geats, is interred.

THE *BEOWULF* MANUSCRIPT

Such is the tale of Beowulf. Although it is written in Ango-Saxon and thus is not, strictly speaking, a Viking myth, there seems no question that it was known to Scandinavians and thus was part of Viking mythology. The Geats came from what is now Sweden; Scyld, the ancestor of Hrothgar, was a ruler of Sweden, so the location of the poem is clearly Scandinavian. At the same time, it demonstrates the close connections that existed in the early Middle Ages between England and Scandinavia.

We are remarkably lucky to know of the poem at all, since it exists in a single manuscript, dating from the late tenth or early eleventh centuries. Considering how easily such manuscripts were destroyed (particularly during the English reformation of the sixteenth century), we're amazingly fortunate to know of its existence.

The manuscript is called the Nowell Codex and is held at Oxford University. J.R.R. Tolkien studied *Beowulf* extensively and made a translation of it that has only recently been published. His scholarly article, "Beowulf: The Monster and the Critics," is considered an important landmark in studies of Anglo-Saxon literature.

The poem is written in Anglo-Saxon in a poetic mode in which the first half of each line alliterates with the second half of the line. Most scholars feel that the poem was first part of an oral tradition and later transcribed for permanent learning.

It also seems clear that the first versions of the poem were pagan, and that later in its life Christian interpolations were added. Grendel, for instance, is described as an offspring of Cain, but there's no reason to think he was originally so described.

CHRISTIAN INFLUENCES

By the time many Viking myths were written down, the chief authors were Christian. Snorri Sturluson was among them, and his account of the Scandinavian gods is tinged with Christian themes.

Heorot

The great hall of Hrothgar in which the first part of the poem's action takes place seems to have had a foundation in reality. Recent excavations at Lejre in Denmark, identified as a possible seat of the Scyldings, Hrothgar's people, show that a great hall was built there during the sixth century, around the time the poem's action occurs.

In any case, the Beowulf poet shows us how centrally important to Viking life was the institution of the hall.

> It came to his mind
> that he would command   a royal building,
> a gabled mead-hall   fashioned by craftsmen,
> which the sons of men   should hear of forever.

Significantly, Heorot is called a mead-hall (the Anglo-Saxon term is *medo-ærn*). Earlier in the poem it is said that the warrior chieftain and Hrothgar's ancestor Scyld Scefing seized mead-benches from enemies.

We can presume that he did not so much take the actual benches on which mead was drunk but instead seized or destroyed the halls of his enemies.

Just as the ship was the most important element in Viking raiding, the hall was the center of Viking settlements. Here the warriors gathered to drink, eat, engage in contests of strength, and listen to a bard recite myths and tales.

BEOWULF AND GRENDEL'S CONTEST

One way to read the account of Beowulf's battle with Grendel in Heorot is that it is a satire of the traditional fights and matches that were the normal source of entertainment in a Norse hall. The watching warriors who dare not interfere with their chieftain's single combat against the monster form a sort of formal audience of this test of strength.

THE TREASURE OF SUTTON HOO

In 1939, archaeologists in East Anglia in England began excavation of one of several large mounds. They discovered almost immediately that they had uncovered a ship burial, one of the most important that had ever been found in the British Isles.

Unfortunately, 1939 was not the best year for archaeological work, since Britain was about to begin a six-year military clash with Germany, during which many parts of Britain would suffer bombings. The Sutton Hoo site was re-covered, and historians and archaeologists spent the next six years with their fingers crossed that the site would be immune from a stray German bomb or rocket.

When investigations resumed in 1946, the scientists found to their delight that although the wooden planks of the ship had rotted away, its shape was almost perfectly preserved in the soil. No body was found, and the general consensus among archaeologists now is that the acidic soil destroyed it.

However, a rich hoard of artifacts was discovered, almost all of which now reside in the British Museum. These include a helmet, sword, and an assortment of jewelry.

One reason for the find's importance is that it confirms in so many respects the account that *Beowulf* and other Viking sagas give of life in Scandinavia and Britain during the early Middle Ages. Contrary to the modern artistic impressions of Vikings wearing helmets with horns on them, their battle helmets probably looked far more like that found at Sutton Hoo: metal flaps hanging from an iron cap, covering the face and ears, with holes for the eyes and mouth. The Sutton Hoo helmet is heavily decorated, and that, combined with the richness of the hoard, suggests the burial was of someone very important. The scholar Henry Chadwick suggested in the 1940s that it may have been Rædwald, king of East Anglia, a proposal that has met with wide (though not complete) agreement.

The site is also noteworthy for the lack of Christian artifacts. In this respect, it is like burial sites from earlier centuries found throughout Scandinavia before the area's conversion. Some scholars have suggested that the kings of East Anglia, who were among the last in Britain to become Christian, made their gravesites particularly rich in contents as a way of demonstrating their independence from Christianity.

Chapter Fourteen

RAGNARÖK: THE END OF THE WORLD

The Vikings had extremely specific beliefs about the end of the world. Of course, eschatology is common to many religions, but the Vikings spelled out the apocalypse in clear detail. They called it Ragnarök, a term used in the *Prose Edda* and in one poem of the *Poetic Edda*. The meaning of the word is not entirely clear, but it seems to mean "the destruction of the gods."

The most complete explanation comes in the *Prose Edda*, when Gylfi asks, "What can you tell me concerning the fate of the gods?"

"Great tidings indeed," replies High.

WINTER AND STRIFE

The beginning of Ragnarök will be signaled by violent changes in the weather. According to the *Völuspá*,

> Dark grows the sun
> And in summer soon
> Come mighty storms.

Snorri says that there will be three winters; the first will be called the Awful Winter in which snow shall drive into every nook and cranny and the air will snap with frost. Winds will tear at frozen limbs and even the sun will be powerless to warm anyone. Between the winters there will be no summer, but all over the nine worlds folk will be wrent by strife. The bonds of kinship will be violated, and children will sin together.

This battle among men is the prologue to the much more serious conflict among the gods that will now occur. Fenriswolf will break free from his bondage and will swallow the sun.

> Axe time, sword time,
> Shields are sundered
> Wind time, wolf time,
> Ere the world falls;
> Nor ever shall men
> Each other spare.

Heimdall, guardian of Bifrost, will raise his horn, Gjallarhorn, and blow, warning the gods of Asgard that Ragnarök is upon them. The earth will tremble, says Snorri, so that "trees shall be torn up from the earth, and the crags fall to ruin."

Jörmungandr will thrash about in the sea, and the waters will spread across Midgard. The ship Naglfar, which is made up of dead men's fingernails and toenails, shall be loose upon the sea, steered by the giant Hrym.

BATTLE OF GIANTS AND GODS

Now Fenriswolf will swell to a gigantic size and place its jaws around the earth. Jörmungandr will blow venom into the air so it rains down upon the world. The giants of Múspell will ride, led by Surtr, surrounded by a burning fire, swords drawn. They will ride across Bifrost, and the bridge will shatter in their wake. They shall pass on to a field called Vígridr, accompanied by Fenriswolf and Jörmungandr.

Loki and Hrym and the frost giants will also go there.

Heimdall's horn will alert all the gods, and they will take council. After this, Odin will ride Sleipnir to Mímir's Well and take council with Mímir's head. As Yggdrasil trembles, filling all the inhabitants of the nine worlds with dread, the Æsir will array themselves for battle and ride forth to Vígridr.

Odin will lead them, armor clad, brandishing his spear Gungnir. On either side of him stand Thor holding Mjollnir and Freyr. Against them are Fenriswolf, who growls and snarls at Odin, saliva dripping from his jaws; Jörmungandr against Thor, its great body thrashing back and forth; and against Freyr is Surtr.

From far below is a great roaring, and the hound Garm bounds up from the Gates of Hel. His destined foe is Tyr the One-Handed, who bravely sacrificed his hand to bind Fenriswolf when the world was young.

The Battles

Thor clashes with the Midgard serpent. Over and over he strikes the beast until at last the wyrm lies dead at his feat. Nine steps Thor takes away from the corpse, and then he too falls lifeless, poisoned by the venom Jörmungandr spewed into the air.

Meanwhile, Odin wrestles with Fenriswolf, his hands holding wide the jaws of the sun swallower. His muscles strain and crack as the wolf tries to snap its mouth shut. A long, low, heart-stopping growl emerges from the back of its throat and runs around the world. Then, in a second, it is over. The wolf swallows the god whole. But Vídarr, god of vengeance, sees what is going forward. He strides forth and places a foot upon Fenriswolf's lower jaw. On that foot is a shoe that is built of the scraps of leather men throw away when they are cobbling shoes. With his hands he seizes the upper jaw of the wolf and rips the wolf in half. Blood pours down like rain across the world.

Meanwhile Loki the Traitor grapples with Heimdall. Many blows do they hew and many wounds do they each inflict. But each will, in the end, fall, slain by the other.

> The sun shall be darkened
> Earth sinks in the sea—
> Glide from the heaven
> The glittering stars
> Smoke-reek rages
> And reddening fire:
> The high heat licks
> Against heaven itself.

THE REBIRTH

The souls of brave warriors fly into the heavens. There are halls to receive them: Brimir, Sindri where dwell the pure in heart. But the oath-breakers and the evil ones are banished to Náströnd, an evil hall, its doors to the north, and through it flow rivers of viper venom.

But in time, the earth shall lift from the waters, verdant and fair, and some gods yet living shall be upon it. Vídarr and Váli shall be there, and the son of Thor, who shall possess Mjollnir. And even Baldr from Hel shall come forth and hold council with those gods that yet live. So the earth shall be renewed, and the race of men shall flourish upon it.

AT THE END

Such is the story told by Snorri Sturluson in the *Prose Edda*. Details are added in the *Völuspá* and other Eddic poems. What the story tells us is that like many other peoples, the Vikings believed in an endless cycle of birth, destruction, and rebirth. This may have been comforting to a people whose lives must often have seemed transient and violent, subject to sudden death or injury.

Though the Vikings were often seen by others in Western Europe as a destructive force, sent to destroy the works of man and God, they were also a deeply civilizing power, who carried their myths and their gods to every corner of the continent and beyond. We owe them a great debt.

GLOSSARY

A

Ægir
God of the sea; possibly a giant.

Æsir
One of the two races of Viking gods (see Vanir). The Æsir include Odin, Thor, Frigg, Baldr, and Tyr.

Alfheim
One of the nine worlds, home of the Light Elves (see Elves), located in the top layer of worlds along with Asgard and Vanaheim.

Andvaranaut
A ring from the hoard of the dragon Fafnir and ultimately from the treasure of Andvari. The ring, like the rest of the treasure, is cursed and brings unhappiness to whoever possesses it.

Andvari
A dwarf, possessor of a great treasure that is eventually taken by Loki and Odin to pay their debt to Hreidmar for slaying his son Otter. However, the dwarf cursed the treasure before they took it.

Angrboda
A giantess and the wife of Loki; mother of Jörmungandr, the World Serpent; Hel; and Fenriswolf (see Loki).

L'Anse aux Meadows
Site of Leif Erikson's first settlement in North America more than 500 years before the voyages of Columbus.

Asgard
One of the nine worlds; dwelling place of the Æsir and Vanir. It is surrounded by a high wall (although incomplete) built by a giant. It also contains Valhalla.

Ask
The first man, made by Odin and his brothers from the wood of an ash tree.

Audhumla
A cow formed from the primal clay of the world, she nourished the giant Ymir. She licked the salt from the rim of Ginnungagap and licked out the form of a man who would become the father of Odin.

B

Baldr
The most beautiful of the Æsir, the offspring of Odin and Frigg. He is killed accidentally by Hödr through the treachery of Loki, for which action Loki is trapped and bound by the gods.

Beowulf

Champion, and later king, of the Geats, a Scandinavian people. He comes to the aid of the Scylding chieftain Hrothgar after a series of attacks on the latter's hall, Heorot. Beowulf defeats the monster Grendel and Grendel's mother but dies many years later after a battle with a dragon.

Bergelmir

The only giant to survive the attack of Odin and his brothers, Vili and Vé. Bergelmir fled and hid and was eventually able to sire more giants who repopulated the frost giants.

Bifrost

The three-colored rainbow bridge that links Midgard and Asgard. It terminates at Himinbjörg, hall of Heimdall, who guards it against possible invasions by the giants.

Billing's daughter

A woman loved by Odin who tricked him, fleeing him and leaving in her place a bitch. The episode prompted the Allfather to meditate on the faithlessness of women.

Borr

Son of Búri (see Búri) and the father of Odin by a woman named Bestla, who in turn was the daughter of a giant.

Bragi

The god of poetry. His daughter Nanna is married to Baldr.

Brísingamen, necklace of
A necklace fashioned by four dwarves and worn by the goddess Freyja after she agreed to sleep with each of the dwarves in turn. The necklace gives the appearance of being on fire.

Brynhild
A Valkyrie and the beloved of Sigurd in the *Völsunga Saga*. Tragically, although Brynhild loves Sigurd above all other men, she knows that the two of them will never be wed. When Sigurd's funeral pyre is lighted, she steps onto it and joins him in death.

Búri
The man who was licked out of the ice of Ginnungagap by Audhumla the cow. He was the father of Borr and the grandfather of Odin.

C

Cnut the Great (c. 995–1035)
Ruler of the Danelaw and later king of a united England as well as Denmark and Norway. Cnut is the greatest of the Danish kings of Britain.

D

Dáinn, Dvalinn, Duneyrr, and Durathrór
Four harts that live in the branches of Yggdrasil, devouring its leaves.

Danelaw

The area of Britain controlled by the Vikings and their descendants from the ninth through the eleventh centuries. It culminated in the reign of Cnute the Great, who ruled a united England, Norway, and Denmark.

Draupnir

An arm ring made by the dwarves for Odin. He places it on the funeral pyre of his son, Baldr.

Dvergatal

A catalog of dwarves' names. Although it is part of the *Völuspá*, many scholars believe it was a later insertion into the poem and not part of the original.

Dwarves

The dwarves of Viking mythology dwell in Svartalfheim. Although they are accounted great craftsmen, they are generally short and ugly with foul tempers. As such they often come into conflict with the gods. The dwarves were fashioned from the body of the primeval giant Ymir.

E

Eikthyrnir

A stag living atop Valhalla. From its horns drips down liquid that flows into Hvergelmir in Niflheim

Eir

Goddess of doctors.

Elves
Elves are rarely seen by humans; they are divided into Light Elves, who live above the ground and love human beings, and Dark Elves, who live below ground and are evil.

Embla
The first woman, made by Odin and his brothers from the wood of an elm tree.

Erik the Red (950–c. 1003)
Norse Viking and father of Leif Erikson, he established the first Viking colonies in Greeland.

F

Fafnir
Son of Hreidmar and brother to Otter and Regin. He lusts after the gold given his father for compensation for the death of Otter. Eventually he steals the gold, but he is turned into a dragon. In this form, he is slain by Sigurd the Volsung.

Farbauti
In some accounts the frost giant who is the father of Loki.

Fenriswolf
One of the children of Loki (the other two are the World Serpent and Hel). Fenriswolf was bound by the gods, but at the coming of Ragnarök, it will break free and swallow Odin whole.

Fensalir
Frigg's hall in Asgard.

Fjalar
One of the two dwarves who killed Kvasir (see Galar; Kvasir).

Forseti
Son of Baldr and Nanna, he renders justice in his hall, Glitnir.

Freyja
Goddess of beauty and love. She drives a chariot pulled by cats and wears the necklace of the Brísingamen. She weeps tears of gold, mourning the loss of her husband Ódr. Her hall is Sessrúmnir at Folkvang in Asgard. She is one of the Vanir sent to the Æsir in the wake of the conflict between the Æsir and the Vanir.

Freyr
One of the Vanir, brother of Freyja, son of Njord. He is associated with virility and with sacral kingship. His beloved is the giantess Gerdr, but to wed her he must give away his magical sword. Lacking it, he will be killed by Surtr at Ragnarök.

Frigg
Goddess of peacemaking and the wife of Odin, she knows the fate of all folk but does not speak it aloud.

Fulla
One of the Æsir, the handmaiden of Frigg, who carries her mistress's possessions in a box fashioned of ash

G

Galar
One of the two dwarves who killed Kvasir (see Fjalar; Kvasir).

Garm
The hound that guards the entrance to Hel.

Gefjun
The goddess of virgins.

Gjallarhorn
The horn kept by Heimdall as he watches Bifrost. He will use it to warn the Æsir of Ragnarök.

Gladsheim
A part of Asgard in which Valhalla is located.

Glasir
The golden trees that stand just outside the doors of Valhalla.

Gleipnir
The chain by which the gods bound Fenriswolf.

Grendel
A monster who attacks Heorot, the hall built by Hrothgar, and slays many of Hrothgar's followers. He later attacks Beowulf but is defeated when the latter wrenches off his arm. He retreats back to his lair where he dies in agony.

Gudrun
Daughter of Giuki, wife of Sigurd the Volsung.

Gungnir
The magical spear carried by Odin. It was brought to him by Loki, who obtained it from the dwarves. It always hits its mark; Odin will carry it with him into the final battle at Ragnarök where he will use it to attack Fenriswolf.

Gunnar
Son of Giuki, brother of Gudrun. He woos and marries Brynhild, although it is actually Sigurd in disguise who does the wooing.

Gunnlöd
Daughter of Suttungr and assigned by him to guard the Mead of Poetry. However, Odin in disguised seduced her and played a trick on her that allowed him to steal much of the mean and return to Asgard with it (see Mead of Poetry; Suttungr).

Guthrum (d. 890)
The Viking chief who negotiated a treaty with Alfred the Great of Wessex establishing the Danelaw. As a condition of the treaty, Guthrum converted to Christianity, taking the name Æthelstan.

Gylfi
The first king of Scandinavia and the principle figure in the *Gylfaginning*, a part of the *Prose Edda*. During the *Gylfaginning*, Gylfi, disguised as Gangleri, goes to Asgard and interviews three mysterious figures about the gods and the nine worlds.

H

Harald Fairhair (c. 850–c. 932)
The first king of Norway, whose reign lasted from c. 872–930.

Heimdall
Guardian of the bridge Bifrost, from where he keeps watch for the coming of Ragnarök. He is the son of nine mothers and is sometimes referred to as the Gold Toothed.

Hel
Both a place and a person. The place is where souls go when they die, although the souls of heroic warriors are brought to Valhalla. Hel, located in the dark, cold world of Niflheim, is presided over by Hel, the youngest daughter of Loki, who is usually depicted as a hag.

Helgi
Son of Sigmund and a leader of the Volsungs.

Heorot
The hall built by Hrothgar that is attacked by Grendel and later defended by Beowulf.

Hermódr
The son of Odin, he travels to Hel to ask for the return of the slain Baldr's soul to Asgard.

Hlidskjalf

The high seat where Odin sits, observing what is occurring in the nine worlds. It is also sometimes depicted as a dwelling, the site of Odin's high seat.

Hreidmar

Father of Otter, Fafnir, and Regin. When Loki killed Otter, Hreidmar demanded compensation in the form of treasure.

Hrothgar

Chief of the Scyldings, builder of Heorot, he calls upon the help of Beowulf when the hall is attacked by the monster Grendel.

Hrungnir

A giant first encountered by Odin and then who fights and loses a duel with Thor. However, a piece of his whetstone is embedded in Thor's skull.

Hugi

A giant whom Thor and Loki meet at Utgarda and who defeats Thor's servant, Thjalfi, in a foot race. In reality, Hugi is the speed of the giant Utgarda's thought.

Huginn

One of two ravens (see Muninn) that sit on Odin's shoulders, he is also called Thought. Each day they fly about the nine worlds and bring him news of what is happening.

Hvergelmir

One of the locations of a root of Yggdrasil, it is found in Niflheim. The word can be translated as "bubbling stream." It is the source of all waters in the world.

Hymir

A giant with whom Thor once went on a fishing expedition. Thor almost caught the World Serpent, but Hymir panicked and cut his line.

Hyrrokkin

A giantess, she pushes out the boat that contains Baldr's funeral pyre. She is one of many giants who attend Baldr's funeral.

I

Idunn

Wife of Bragi and keeper of magical apples that keep the gods ever young. She and her apples were kidnapped by the giant Thiazi with the contrivance of Loki.

J

Jörmungandr

The World Serpent, offspring of Loki and Angrboda. When Odin created Midgard, he threw the serpent into the sea surrounding the world. There the serpent curled around the world, biting its own tail.

Jötunheim
One of the nine worlds; home of the giants. It is dominated by the fortress of Utgard.

K

Kvasir
A wise man created by the gods at the end of the war between the Æsir and the Vanir. In the course of his travels through the world to resolve disputes, he encountered two dwarves who killed him and brewed the Mead of Poetry from his body.

L

Leif Erikson
Son of Erik the Red. He and his followers traveled west as far as Newfoundland and possibly the mouth of the St. Lawrence Seaway. They named the land they discovered Vinland.

Logi
Apparently a giant whom Thor and Loki meet at Utgard and who defeats Loki in an eating contest. In reality, Logi is wild fire.

Loki
A trickster who is either a god, according to some sources, or a giant according to others. He is the father, by the giantess Angrboda, of Jörmungandr, the World Serpent; Fenriswolf; and Hel. Disguised as a mare, Loki gave birth to Sleipnir, Odin's eight-legged horse. For

conniving the death of Baldr, most beloved of the gods, Loki is bound with a serpent above his face that continuously drips venom on him.

M

Magni
Thor's son by the giantess Jarnsaxa. Having inherited the strength of both his parents, he is capable of feats of prowess when he is only a baby.

Mead of Poetry
A marvelous mead brewed by the dwarves Fjalar and Galar from the body of Kvasir, a wise man created by the Æsir and Vanir. Through trickery, Odin obtained some of the mead and brought it to Asgard.

Mengloth
The object of the hero Svipdag's love, she lives in Giant Land in a fortress guarded by the giant Fjolsvid. Svipdag succeeds in gaining her love.

Midgard
Middle-earth, one of the nine worlds. It is here that human beings live. The gods often travel to Midgard either to seek adventure or to interact with its inhabitants. Midgard is surrounded by a vast sea, in which rests Jörmungandr, the World Serpent.

Mímir
A wise god, a member of the Æsir. In the wake of the conflict between the Æsir and the Vanir, Mímir was given to the latter as a hostage.

However, feeling they had got the worst of the hostage exchange, the Vanir cut off his head. Odin retrieved it and preserved it so ever after he had the advice of the wise Mímir.

Mjollnir
The hammer of Thor, made by the dwarves. Its short handle is due to a mistake in its making. With it, Thor slays giants, the foes of the Æsir and Vanir. It was stolen by the giant Thrym but recovered by Thor with the assistance of Loki.

Muninn
One of two ravens (see Huginn) that sit on Odin's shoulders, he is also called Memory. Each day they fly about the nine worlds and bring the god news of what is happening.

Múspell
Prior to the creation of the world, one of two realms. Múspell lay to the south and was fiery and hot. After the creation of the cosmos, it became Múspellsheimr, one of the nine worlds.

Múspellsheimr
One of the nine worlds, a place of fire. It is guarded by the giant Surtr, who at the end of the world will defeat the god Freyr (see Ragnarök).

N

Naglfar
A ship built entirely of human nails, which will be launched at the beginning of Ragnarök. It will be captained by the giant Hrym.

Nanna

Wife of Baldr who dies of grief at his funeral and is thus burned on the same pyre as her husband. In Saxo Grammaticus's *Gesta Danorum* she is a human being loved by both Baldr and Hödr.

Narfi

The son of Loki, who is killed by his brother, Váli, after the latter is transformed by Odin into a wolf. Narfi's guts are used to bind Loki.

Náströnd

The hall to which the souls of murderers and oath-breakers are banished after Ragnarök.

Nidavellir

The home of the Dark Elves; see Svartalfheim.

Nidhogg

The dragon that perpetually gnaws on the roots of Yggdrasil. It also chews the corpses of those guilty of murder, rape, or oath-breaking.

Niflheim

One of the two realms before the creation of the world. It was in the north and was dark and cold and the source of eleven rivers, which poured their waters into the Ginnungagap (the Yawning Gap) between Múspellsheimr and Niflheim. After the creation of the cosmos, Niflheim became one of the nine worlds and the seat of Hel.

Njord
Father of Freyja and Freyr and god of boats and trading. He was one of the Vanir who was sent to live with the Æsir after the conflict between the two groups of gods.

Noatun
A hall, the home of the god Njord.

O

Odin
The Allfather. Father and chief of the gods of Asgard. He is the god of ecstasy and poetry as well as the god of battle. He receives half of those who die in battle. The heroes he welcomes to the hall of Valhalla in Asgard. He possesses the Mead of Poetry and hung on the World Tree, Yggdrasil, for nine nights to gain the knowledge of runes. He will die at Ragnarök by being swallowed whole by the wolf Fenriswolf.

Ódr
The lost husband of Freyja, for whom she weeps golden tears.

Oseberg ship
A Viking ship discovered at Slagen, Norway, in 1903. It is one of the most well preserved and complete examples of a Viking ship extant. It dates from the ninth century.

P

Poetic Edda
A compilation of poetry related to the doings of gods and heroes. For a complete list of the contents of the *Poetic Edda*, see Chapter 4. The poems are by different people and were written at different times, but the most important version, the Codex Regius, was compiled in the thirteenth century. It was used as a source by Snorri Sturluson in his *Prose Edda*.

Prose Edda
Written by Snorri Sturluson in the first part of the thirteenth century, this work contains a Prologue, the *Gylfaginning*, the *Skáldskaparmál*, and the *Háttatal*. The *Prose Edda* is one of the most important sources of information about Scandinavian mythology and literature.

R

Ragnarök
The Scandinavian myth of the end of the world. During Ragnarök there will be battles between the gods and monsters such as the World Serpent and Fenriswolf. From the ruin of the earth that is caused by these struggles, there will arise a new world.

Ratatoskr
The squirrel that lives in the branches of Yggdrasil. It carries messages from the eagle, Vethirfölnir, which sits at the top of the tree, and Nidhogg, the dragon that gnaws at the tree's roots.

Regin
The tutor of Sigurd, he sought to use the Volsung's power selfishly toward his own ends. When Sigurd discovered this, he killed Regin.

Ríg
A god who sires the various social groups of men by sleeping with three different women. The first gives birth to the ancestors of thralls; the second to the ancestors of freemen; and the third to the ancestors of noble warriors.

Rollo (c. 863–c. 940)
Viking leader to whom the Frankish king Charles the Simple gave a large grant of land in what is now called Normandy (after the Northmen). In return, Rollo put his followers at the service of the Frankish state.

Roskva
A servant of Thor.

Runes
A form of writing often used for magical inscriptions, widespread throughout the Germanic world. The runic alphabet is known as the futhark from the first six letters in it (the "th" sound is represented by one of two alternate letters call the thorn and the eth). Odin learned the secret of runes by hanging for nine nights from the branches of Yggdrasil.

Rus
The name given to Vikings who crossed the Baltic and raided the east as far as Constantinople. They later established the Kievan state, which eventually evolved into Russia.

S

Saxo Grammaticus (c. 1150–c. 1220)
A twelfth-century chronicler, author of *Gesta Danorum*. He provides an important source for the history and mythology of the Viking age.

Sif
Thor's wife. Her pride is her beautiful golden hair, which Loki stole once as a joke.

Siggeir
King of Gothland and husband of Signy, daughter of Volsung and Ljod, the giant's daughter. He later betrayed the Volsungs and was eventually killed by Volsung and Sigmund.

Sigmund
Son of Volsung and Ljod, the giant's daughter. He was treacherously attacked by his brother-in-law but survived and sired Sigurd.

Sigurd
Son of Sigmund, beloved of Brynhild, husband of Gudrun. He is the hero of the *Völusunga Saga*.

Sigyn

The wife of Loki. After his binding, when a venomous serpent is suspended above him so its poison drips on his face, she catches the poison in a wooden bowl. When the bowl is full, she empties it into a rocky basin, and Loki writhes in agony beneath the still-dripping venom.

Sinfjotli

Signy's son by her brother Sigmund.

Sjofn

Goddess of love and lovers.

Skathi

Wife of Njord. She is a giantess and the patroness of hunting. In some accounts Njord killed her father, Thiazi, and married her by way of compensation. (In the story of Idunn's apples, it is Thor who kills Thiazi.) She later left Njord and married Odin, by whom she had many children. When the gods bind Loki, it is Skathi who places a snake above his face so that it perpetually drips venom upon him.

Skidbladnir

A ship fashioned for Freyr by the dwarves. When not in use it can be folded so it is no bigger than a piece of parchment.

Skrymir

See Utgard.

Skuld

One of the three norns who live at the Well of Urdr beneath one of the roots of Yggdrasil. Her name translates as "future." She is also possibly a Valkyrie.

Sleipnir

The eight-legged horse ridden by Odin. Sleipnir was conceived by Loki while he was in the shape of the mare in order to distract that magical horse Svadilfari. Hermódr rides Sleipnir to Hel after Baldr's death to beg for the return of the god.

Snorri Sturluson (1179–1241)

Poet and politician, author of the *Prose Edda*, *Heimskringla*, and probably *Egil's Saga*. His work is one of the most important sources for our knowledge of Viking mythology.

Suttungr

In revenge for the murder of his father Gilling by the two dwarves Fjalar and Galar, Suttungr obtained from them the Mead of Poetry. Much of the mead was stolen from him by Odin in disguise (see Mead of Poetry; Fjalar; Galar).

Svadilfari

A magical horse that helps a giant to build the wall around Asgard. Because the horse works all night as well as all day, the giant comes close to completing the wall, which would have required the gods to give him Freyja, the sun, and the moon. However, Loki, disguised as a mare, distracted Svadilfari, and the wall was not completed.

Svartalfheim
One of the nine worlds; home of the dwarves.

Svipdag
Son of the seeress Groa, he was destined to seek out the beautiful woman Mengloth and declare his love for her. Despite her being guarded by a giant, he succeeded, and they were united in love.

T

Thiazi
A giant, father of Skathi, who is the wife of the Vanir Njord. Thiazi is behind the theft of Idunn's apples, which he manages with the help of Loki.

Thjalfi
A servant of Thor. He was defeated at a race (through trickery) during a visit by Thor and Loki to the fortress of Utgarda-Loki in Giant Land.

Thökk
A giantess, the one being in all the nine worlds who refuses to weep for the slain Baldr, thus condemning him to remain in Hel. Some of the gods suspect that Thökk is really Loki in disguise, bent on frustrating the wishes of Odin and Frigg.

Thor
The god of thunder, son of Odin. With his hammer, Mjollnir, he rides his chariot pulled by the goats Tooth-gnasher and Tooth-gritter. His hammer alone can protect the Æsir and Vanir from the giants.

Thrym
A king of the giants who steals Thor's hammer, Mjollnir. Through trickery, Loki and Thor get the hammer back, and Thor uses it to kill Thrym.

Tyr
The god of heroism and law. He is one-handed, having lost one of his hands in the struggle to bind Fenriswolf.

U

Ull
Stepson of Thor, his mother is Sif. He is skilled with a bow and is a notable warrior.

Urdr
One of the Norns, she is also sometimes known as Fate. She resides at the Well of Urdr beneath one of the roots of Yggdrasil.

Utgard
The castle and realm ruled by the giant Utgarda-Loki.

Utgarda-Loki
A giant to whose stronghold Thor and Loki paid a visit. The giant disguised himself as another giant named Skrymir and played various tricks on them that enraged Thor.

V

Valhalla
Odin's hall of heroes in Asgard, where the souls of half those of die heroically in battle are welcomed and reside until the coming of Ragnarök.

Vali
The son of Odin and Rind.

Váli
The son of Loki. Odin transforms him into a wolf that tears out his brother, Narfi's, guts. The gods then use those guts to bind Loki.

Valkyries
Warlike women who escort the souls of heroes who fall in battle to Valhalla and, once there, wait upon them.

Vanaheim
One of the nine worlds; home of the Vanir.

Vanir
One of two races of Viking gods (see Æsir). The Vanir included Njord, Freyr, Freyja, and other gods only incidentally mentioned. It is possible that the cult of the Vanir was connected to fertility rituals.

Var
Goddess of contracts and agreements.

Verdandi

One of the three Norns who live at the Well of Urdr beneath the root of Yggdrasil. Her name means "present" or "becoming."

Víðarr

Sometimes called the silent god, he will use his shoe to kill Fenriswolf during Ragnarök. He is the god of vengeance.

Vígriðr

The site of the final battle between gods and monsters during Ragnarök.

Vili and Vé

The brothers of Odin, who helped him destroy the giant Ymir and use the giant's body to create the world.

Vinland

Land discovered in North America by Leif Erikson. It was probably around the mouth of the St. Lawrence Seaway.

Volsung

Leader of the Volsung clan, father of Sigmund and Signy.

Völuspá

A poem about the creation of the world; part of the *Poetic Edda*.

W

Well of Urdr
A well in Asgard that lies beneath a root of Yggdrasil, the World Tree. The gods gather at the well each day to pronounce their judgments.

Woden
German form of Odin.

Y

Yggdrasil
The World Tree of Norse mythology. It is an ash whose trunk and roots spread throughout the nine worlds. One root is in Asgard at the Well of Urdr; a second is in Niflheim over the well Mímisbrunnr; and a third in Jötunheim in the place where Ginnungagap, the Yawning Void, formerly existed (see Chapter 5).

Ymir
The giant who was formed by the ice in Ginnungagap in the beginning of the world. The world was shaped from his body by Odin and his brothers. Ymir is described in the *Prose Edda* as "the father of all frost giants."

BIBLIOGRAPHY

Allan, Tony, *The Vikings: Life, Myth, and Art*. New York: Barnes and Noble, 2004.

Bellows, Henry Adams, *The Poetic Edda*. Princeton: Princeton University Press, 1936.

Beowulf: A Dual-Language Edition. Trans. Howell D. Chickering, Jr. Garden City, NY: Anchor Books, 1977.

Craigie, W.A., *The Religion of Ancient Scandinavia*. New York: Pyrrhus Press, reprinted 2014.

Crossley-Holland, Kevin, *The Norse Myths*. New York: Pantheon, 1980.

Davidson, H.R. Ellis, *Gods and Myths of Northern Europe*. New York: Penguin, 1965.

Ferguson, Robert, *The Vikings: A History*. New York: Penguin, 2009.

Graham-Campbell, James, and Dafydd Kidd, *The Vikings*. New York: William Morrow, 1980.

Pye, Michael, *The Edge of the World: A Cultural History of the North Sea and the Transformation of Europe*. London: Pegasus, 2016.

Roesdahl, Else, *Vikings*, revised edition. New York: Penguin, 1998.

Rosenberg, Donna, *World Mythology: An Anthology of the Great Myths and Epics*, 2nd edition. Lincolnwood, IL: NTC Publishing Group, 1994.

Smiley, Jane, ed., *The Sagas of Icelanders*. New York: Penguin, 2000.

Sturluson, Snorri, *The Prose Edda*. Trans. Jesse L. Byock. New York: Penguin, 2005.

Wernick, Robert, and the Editors of Time-Life Books, *The Vikings: The Seafarers*. Alexandria, VA: Time-Life Books, 1979.

INDEX

ABOUT THE AUTHOR

Peter Archer holds an MA from the University of Toledo and an MLitt in medieval history from the University of St. Andrews. He first formed a connection to the Vikings when he visited L'Anse aux Meadows, site of the first Viking settlement in North America, in 1967. While teaching classes at Eastern New Mexico University, he lectured on mythology and folklore. He is currently an associate editor for Adams Media and lives in Massachusetts in a 200-year-old house filled with books and cats.